TREVOR STUBBS lived the first nineteen years of his life in Northampton, England. A fortunate choice of a secondary modern school and membership of an inspiring church youth group set him up well for eventual success in his A levels and a place at King's College, London to study theology.

Three years voluntary service as a teacher in Papua New Guinea followed and after a year in St Augustine's College, Canterbury he was ordained in Wakefield Cathedral in 1974. As a curate in Heckmondwike, West Yorkshire he met and married Tina. A three-year appointment in Warwick, Queensland, Australia came next before a return to Yorkshire and an incumbency in Leeds.

Moving to Dorset in 1989, Trevor served in two parishes over the next twenty years and then, finally, took up a post teaching in South Sudan.

Retirement near Bristol saw the beginning of his writing career. Trevor is the author of four books in the White Gates series which he describes as 'fantasy fiction with a spiritual heart'.

The *Flip* trilogy comes under the titles of *On the Edge*, *Beyond the Horizon* and *The Daisychain*.

Trevor and Tina have three children and two grandchildren.

I0592905

FROM THE SAME AUTHOR

In this series:

Flip! On the Edge

Flip! Beyond the Horizon

Flip! The Daisychain

In the White Gates series:

The Kicking Tree

Ultimate Justice

Winds & Wonders

The Spark

From the author of the
White Gates Adventures series

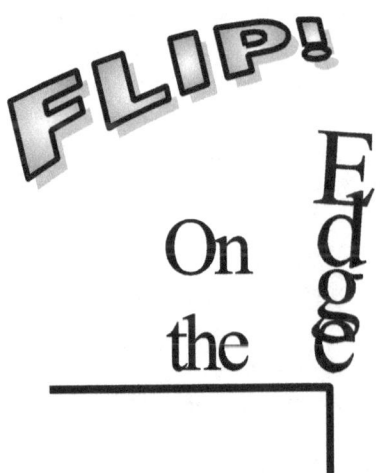

FLIP!
On the Edge

TEETERING ON THE EDGE OF REASON,
TRUTH, POWER AND REALITY ITSELF...

TREVOR STUBBS

THE
LISTENING
PEOPLE

The Listening People
15 Cleeve Grove
Keynsham,
Bristol, BS31 2HF

Email: author@trevorstubbs.co.uk
Web: www.trevorstubbs.co.uk

ISBN 978 0-9550100-1-9

British Library Cataloguing in Publication Data.
A catalogue record for this book is available from the British Library.

THE
LISTENING
PEOPLE

In gratitude for the young people and the youth leaders of St Peter & St Paul's, Abington, Northampton among whom I grew up in the 1960s. They befriended and encouraged me to become more than I could have dreamed.

"One of the troubles of our age is that habits of thought cannot change as quickly as techniques, with the result that, as skill increases, wisdom fades."

Bertrand Russell, *Has Man a Future* (1961)

1

That lunchtime, Nadia felt life was reasonably good. Despite the wind, the mid-March sky was cloudless and the sun cast sharp shadows across the stained concrete slabs and brave green weeds which exploited the cracks. St Paul's didn't look quite so bad when nature broke through. But, whatever the weather, life was tough for Nadia Simpson – she had no mother and her father depended on her to look after him. She knew he loved her... well, when he wasn't drunk and had no idea what time of day it was.

The Year 10 English test had gone particularly well. There was no way she was going to get more than a pass, of course – she wasn't that good – but a pass was all she needed.

Two more summers and she would leave school and go on to do the childcare apprenticeship she had set her heart on. She loved children. Being an only one and not having any cousins meant there were never any at home; it was just her and her dad. So if she wanted to be with children, it would have to be with other people's and that had the added advantage of being paid.

Nadia fought her way up the blustery street singing to herself and was quite oblivious to the lumbering approach of

Dean Sharman, a local hooligan from her street who appeared to see it as one of his purposes in life to torment her. He ran up behind her and gave her a solid push which caught Nadia unawares. Grabbing her school bag, Sharman headed off down a side street. Nadia swore.

She gathered herself together and chased after Demon Dean, as she called him. She knew she could catch him. He wasn't very fit and was shorter than she was. As she got within reach of him, Dean lobbed the bag over a garden gate and kept going, breathing heavily. Nadia took a mental note of the gate but continued her pursuit. She was going to... well, she wasn't quite sure what she was going to do when she caught him, but catch him she would. If she could just take that horrid smirk off his face...

Then it happened! The world turned on its head. The street spun as if in a spin dryer. The sunlit painted redbrick houses mingled with the greens of the growing things, and the blue of the sky. Her shouts seemed to become absorbed into a thick wall of silence. All colour disappeared - she was immersed in a strange grey world. A slope of darker grey extended up from left to right, to which Nadia seemed stuck. Her feet didn't work - she had ceased running. But where were her feet? She couldn't make them out.

Her attention was drawn to a line of flat black blobs that glided past her in the direction she was looking. Where was she? What had happened to the world?

Down beside her, to the left of the slope, she noticed a spinning ball where the grey was tinged with faint colour. It swirled like water going down a plughole. As she looked at it, the ball grew in size and then, at last, she saw her feet but she had no power over them as they were stretched out, inexorably drawn to the vortex. And then, as Nadia uttered an inaudible scream, the whole of her was sucked through.

Finally, just as suddenly, she was back in the street sitting in a puddle. Dean had gone. Nadia swore, got to her feet, swore again, retrieved her bag and went home.

She didn't want to admit it to herself but she had been frightened. Something had happened to her and she didn't know what it was.

2

On a crisp morning in the Scottish Highlands, visitors arrived in sports cars, luxury four-by-fours and even chauffeur-driven limousines. As well as its stunning scenery, the Inverlochie Estate was noted for its game; rich men from around the world came to shoot things – deer, grouse, pheasants or anything else that came in range. But today's guests had not come for the sport. To the untrained eye, apart from the arrogance of wealth, they appeared a varied bunch. Some wore suits, others knitted jumpers and corduroy trousers or jeans, but they all had one thing in common: each wore, somewhere on their person, the form of a simple daisy. Cuff links, tie-pins, buttons, shoe buckles, earrings, embroidered caps, shirts and handkerchiefs, all included subtle forms of this humble flower.

"Good morning, Commander," said Donald Padget in a deliberately clipped American accent.

"Good morning," replied Audra McBlair. "Have you had a good journey?"

"Apart from the ridiculous boarding procedures at Dulles International," snapped the portly but smart business man. "It tires me that I have to travel 'under the radar' despite possessing my own jet."

"Yes, but security demands it at this stage. Don't worry, the Cause recognises your contribution, comrade. It won't be long," she chided him with a smile. "Airport terminals will be a thing of the past for you."

"Thank you, Commander. I think I can wait. In the meantime, it is good to be back in my own castle."

Over an opulent lunch, ten men and Audra McBlair discussed progress. Daisychain had many people of influence around the world. They were ready to act; the plans were taking shape... And current governments had no idea what was happening.

"I have one more key ingredient," smiled Padget, as he addressed the gathering. "I have identified a source of power as yet untapped. And I am on the brink of delivering it to the Daisychain. Commander, gentlemen, what would you say if I told you that not only is there a fifth dimension to reality but that we are also on the way to gaining exclusive access to it?"

"A fifth dimension?" queried McBlair. "Beyond the four of space and time?"

"Precisely. You may well look amazed but it is true."

"If there is another dimension, then it must be controlled," said a man in a gruff French accent. "An uncontrolled dimension is unthinkable."

"I agree," affirmed Padget. "We must have control. But,

not only will we have control, we are going to be able to use this for our own ends. Currently, only a handful of people visit it and they are nearly all teenagers who have no idea what is happening to them. The only place in the world doing significant research into the phenomenon – apart from an excuse of an institution in the States – is the Winterford Clinic in London, a place I have bought into. Without my investment, it would have closed. The professor there is so set on his science that he is blind to its implications. He will go along with anyone who will give him the funds he needs."

"Good." said McBlair, "Once again, it seems, our ineffective so-called world leaders are failing to see what is so obviously a must-have power. Not us." Padget smiled away his surge of pride. "Well done, Donald. We shall procure this capacity. How long before you can deliver, comrade?"

"The professor assures me he is on the cusp of completing his studies but you know what these scientists are like. They have a tendency to prevaricate until they have tested everything to death. Given a few threats like the withdrawal of funding, I am confident he will deliver within a very few months."

"I can give you no more than six," said McBlair, firmly. "Then our takeover begins."

"I know. I can... I *shall* deliver, Commander."

3

At home in St Paul's, Nadia was woken at half past midnight by the crash of her front door and the loud slurred cursing of her father as he fell over the recycling box. In colourful language, the man vowed to kill his daughter for putting it there and Nadia sighed. She turned over and did her best to ignore the expletives but she couldn't, so she shouted a few of her own, adding, "It's maths paper four tomorrow, Dad. Let me get some sleep."

"Hark at la-di-da, my too-righteous daughter," Johnny Simpson drawled. "Who brings in the keep in this house Miss Goody Two-Shoes?"

Nadia had learned to take charge of most of the weekly disability benefit her dad got. If she didn't, neither of them would eat.

Johnny Simpson staggered into the bathroom. Nadia was vaguely aware of the sound of running water as sleep overcame her annoyance.

The following day was wet but Nadia wrapped herself up and rolled into school ready for her maths exam. Maths was important – the same as English, she needed a pass. What happened to the rest of the subjects didn't matter that much but, without a pass in English and maths, she wouldn't be allowed to get onto the GCSE course that would qualify her for the childcare apprenticeship.

At one o'clock Nadia put down her pen and wiped her brow. She had done it – or at least her sweaty pen had. The thing with maths was that you had a good idea when you had got it right. Not only had she remembered her formulae, but she had also managed to finish the paper!

After the exam, her various school buddies set off in different directions for lunch but Nadia had no lunch and no money to buy any if she and her father were to eat that evening. She took several gulps of water before walking across the city in the direction of the Downs. It had stopped raining and Nadia did not want to go home.

As she climbed out of Bristol city centre, the houses became less dense and their front gardens better kept, before eventually terminating in the wide road that separated them from the Clifton Downs that surmounted the hill. A couple of football matches were taking place on two of the many marked out pitches. Nadia watched the football for a bit before sauntering across the grass to the far side where there was a solitary ice cream van and a line of cars that indicated the edge of the Clifton Gorge with its stunning view of the historic suspension bridge.

Nadia leaned against the fence and peered down at the assortment of wildflowers that enjoyed the seclusion of the cliff top. She recalled that this place was popular among those who wanted to commit suicide. Only a month before, a teenager not much older than herself had ended her life here. The event had sent shock waves through Nadia. *What does it take to lead people to do that?*

Just then, as if summoned by Nadia's thoughts, the sun came out, bathing her with its bright rays – but the sky on the far side of the gorge remained leaden with heavy dark clouds. Over there, not so very far away, it began to rain while Nadia was still standing in bright sunlight. And then, above and right down into the gorge, appeared a fantastic rainbow. Wow! Nadia could never remember seeing a rainbow quite so stunningly beautiful.

And then, wham! Nadia's world suddenly turned topsy-turvy again. The raindow's colours streaked into a whirl and were replaced by the flat grey board that sloped up to the right. *What the hell is happening to me?* thought Nadia. *Surely I haven't plunged over the gorge.* She prepared herself to crash into the rocks below, but she landed gently. She found herself laying on the pavement beside the fence – the safe side of the fence.

"Are you all right?"

Nadia looked up to see a woman bending over her. She had a small dog that found her interesting.

"I'm... OK," muttered Nadia. She was in shock. Why was she on the floor?

A man in a black tracksuit and football boots trotted over. He had been running the line for the nearest football match. "Someone collapsed?" he enquired.

Nadia pulled herself to her feet. The uninvited attention was unwelcome. "I'm OK. Just leave me alone," she demanded. But by then the match had been called to a halt and a coach was descending on her with a first aid bag. "Leave me alo—"

This time the flip was far more intense. Nadia was in the grey world with sounds beyond the distant jumble of voices somewhere in a different place. The slope was steep but Nadia adhered to it without slipping down. Large black round shapes were drifting along the slope and down to her left was the spinning disc like a vortex. She fixed her gaze on it and then her feet came up and she saw them pass in front of her eyes and disappear down the whirlpool. Then her whole body slid through and she was lying on the pavement again, staring up at a circle of anxious-looking faces and a blue sky.

The coach refused to let her get up. Within what seemed no more than a couple of minutes, green-overalled paramedics were lifting her onto a stretcher before wiring her up to machines in the back of their ambulance. Nadia was their prisoner and no amount of protesting seemed to gain her release. In truth, Nadia wasn't making much sense – the shock had affected her more deeply than she realised.

4

Inside the A&E department of the Bristol Royal Infirmary, the questions began. What drugs had she taken?

"I ain't taken no bleeding drugs. I don't do drugs," protested Nadia, vehemently.

"Glad to hear it," said a young-looking doctor, softly. "I was asking about prescription medicines."

"Oh, sorry. No. None."

"You've had a bit of a shock. Can you tell us what happened?"

"I was looking at the rainbow, and then I was in this grey world – no beautiful rainbow there – then I was on the floor. I don't know how I got there... Look, I wasn't, like, trying to jump or anything. I wouldn't do that. My dad needs me... Are we done here? Dad will be wondering where I've got to."

"We want to make sure you're safe. All your vital signs seem to be in order. When did you last eat?"

"Breakfast."

"What did you have for breakfast?" asked the doctor, with a look of concern.

"Cereal... and a slice of bread."

"Anything for lunch?"

"Nah. Generally manage without lunch."

"How old are you?" asked the doctor, flipping through his notes.

"Fourteen," supplied Nadia.

"At fourteen you need to eat."

"Well, yeah. Me and Dad usually get stuff for tea."

"Do you often go without anything in the middle of the day?"

"It depends."

"Depends on what?"

"Money, of course. I used to have stuff for lunch when I didn't eat breakfast, but Miss said that breakfast is important – especially if you're sitting exams – so I've been having breakfast instead. Now, can I go?"

The young doctor brightened. "I don't usually do this for my patients – and I'd be pleased if you didn't tell anyone," he indicated the nurses at the desk over his shoulder. "But doctor says to take this 'prescription'," he handed her a five-pound note, "down to the café in the entrance and get yourself something to eat. Then you can go home."

Nadia stared at him. "What?"

"All that I can find wrong with you is a lack of calories... Take it. Now go!"

"I can't–"

"You can or I'll keep you here until they serve dinner."

"OK. Thanks, doc." Nadia relented and accepted the money.

"That way. Down to the end of the corridor and turn left. Follow the signs."

'Patient discharged,' he wrote on the clipboard as he watched Nadia leave A&E. He had taken a liking to her – she was rough and ready but honest. They had tried to contact the father but he had come across people like her before – teenagers who were the main carers in a family. At least this girl didn't appear to be looking after younger siblings as well as her father. He resolved to be firm. If the father got hold of the money he had given the girl, none of it would go on food for her. He put down his clipboard and ran for the stairs; he arrived at the bottom well before the lift.

Nadia had no intention of going to the café in the hospital, of course. Five pounds could help her get something a bit decent for her dad. In the main corridor, she turned away from the café sign to find the way out, but as she rounded the corner there was the doctor.

"Café's that way," he said.

"Yeah, I..."

"If you really want to help your dad, you need to look after yourself first. Come—"

But, before either of them could say any more, Nadia

14

suddenly dropped and then, there she was on the floor. This was not like anything the doctor had seen before - this was no ordinary collapse. Her pulse was perfect, her breathing fine, her eyes betrayed no sign of a fit. The first words Nadia said to him when she came round were: "It's so dull in there. Safe but dull."

"In where?" asked the doctor. He was suspicious. Was this yet another case of young people taking a flip into another dimension? To him, as a scientist, it didn't seem as strange as it did to the usual person in the street. This wasn't the first person who had presented like this - but it was the first time he had actually witnessed flipping. "Nadia, I really can't let you go home," he said.

"Yeah. Course you can. I ain't done nothing—"

"You've flipped three times in one day. Out there, there is a lot of traffic. How do you intend to get to St Paul's?"

"Walk. I ain't no slouch," protested Nadia.

"I can see that. But if you were me, would you let someone go knowing they stood a real risk of falling under a bus...? Come on, we'll find your dad."

"OK. He won't hear of me staying."

"He can take you home when he gets here," said the doctor.

"Some hopes. He's most likely out of his head by now."

And so it turned out. And Nadia was obliged to spend the

night in the hospital. Although she tried very hard not to, she flipped again in front of an efficient-looking nurse who instantly became really attentive. She didn't let Nadia feel a fraud being there. The food wasn't bad either. She tucked into a pretty good meal – well, two really because there was a spare one that had come for someone who had been transferred off the ward and the sister asked her if she wanted more.

☆ ☆ ☆

The following day the doctor turned up to see her. He had a stocky woman with him who had expressed an interest in Nadia's case. The woman turned out to be from the London School of Medicine where she was part of the Post-Puberty Medical Research department.

Nadia didn't take to her. The woman's face was big; she reminded Nadia of a monster woman in a horror movie she had seen and it had given her nightmares for a week. The monster wore a chunky necklace and a huge scrunchy around a tight bun at the back of her head. What Nadia noticed particularly were the earrings. They didn't go with the rest. They were delicate pendants – golden chains of daisies which looked too delicate and girly for this big woman in her fifties.

The woman asked lots of questions. Finally, she turned to the doctor and said. "I think Miss Simpson would be a perfect candidate for the Winterford Clinic in St John's Wood."

"I doubt she could pay for private—"

"No. It would be completely free," interrupted the woman, with an air of finality. "You see, it is a research facility and the professor there is looking for new subjects." She turned to Nadia. "How would you like to go to London and be part of a cutting-edge research project into the fifth dimension?" She wore a sickly expression on her large face which Nadia didn't fail to see.

"Nah. Thanks. Kind of you but I reckon I'll give it a miss. I got to stay to look after me dad."

"Well. The offer is there," persisted the woman. "You'll not only be helping yourself but other sufferers like you."

"Other kids, who have this fifth thing?"

"Yes."

"I don't know nobody else who's got this," said Nadia. The thought of meeting other people with the same problem was severely tempting. But, then, it was a non-starter, wasn't it? "Where's me dad?" she asked.

"The social worker says—" began the doctor.

"Social worker?!" said Nadia, really alarmed. "What's it got to do with a social worker?"

"Look, Nadia," said the doctor, "you need care. That's why I detained you yesterday. As you said, your dad was too... inconvenienced—"

"You mean drunk!"

"Too drunk to attend the hospital. The social worker will look after you until—"

"I ain't going to no children's home! Or foster parents! I've done that and it don't work." Nadia felt the chair move and then she was stuck on the forty-five-degree slope with the black blobs she was beginning to hate. She looked for the whirlpool and slid through it.

Back on the floor at the feet of the monster woman she felt small and stupid. But she knew what she had to do. If it was a choice of a foster home or this clinic with other people who shared her problem, it was a no-brainer.

"OK. I'll go to this London place... but only when I've seen my dad."

"Of course," said the doctor. "We do need him to give his consent."

Faced with the prospect of losing her anyway, Nadia knew that he would agree to her going. He'd do what she asked him to. And then, if he didn't cope, they'd take him into somewhere – they would have to.

5

Outside the Winterford clinic, Roxanne Battie got out of her social worker's car and pressed the buzzer on the keypad as directed. She didn't like the look of the place one little bit. A curt voice answered. Roxanne gave her name and the gates began to open. Once inside, they closed again behind them. Roxanne felt like her life had ended. Any freedom she might have been able to look forward to had now vanished. A heavy oak door admitted them.

The social worker signed the necessary papers and Roxanne was left in the care of the housekeeper, a Mrs Brean, who, it became quickly apparent, didn't care for young people. She ushered Roxanne into the presence of her boss and became syrupy-sweet.

"Well Miss Battie, I do hope you settle in quickly," explained an odd-looking man who had introduced himself as Professor Williams. "You are our first resident subject and I must say this is an exciting time for us. You are soon to be joined by a Miss Simpson. She's the same age as you and manifests the same highly interesting condition. Together you and hopefully more teenagers in the future will help us find a lasting cure for this er... tendency to... er, be transported into a fifth dimension." He beamed. "Interesting. Fascinating. I have been working on this over the past few years and now I have, at last, the opportunity to experiment on... I mean research this phenomenon with my own resident subjects."

On that first night, Roxanne decided she was not going to stay. Although she had kept a few friends in her year at school and still communicated with them, she had not been allowed to bring her phone; she was completely cut off in a soulless cold mansion in a part of London she had never been to before. She found her room was too high up for her to escape through the window or she would have gone that very night.

The arrival of Nadia Simpson the next day prevented her plotting other ways to get out. Nadia was OK and they palled up. They found they had a lot in common.

☆ ☆ ☆

Two weeks later, however, things came to a horrifying head. The professor's initial enthusiasm had become tempered by Roxanne's failure to flip at all. She had been doing it every day up until coming to the Winterford and now, for some weird reason, everything had stopped. Instead of being happy for her and arranging for her to leave, the professor had become cross. It had been evident from the start that he was not interested at all in his patients as people – it was all about the research.

"Miss Battie, this place does not run on fresh air, you know," he complained.

"Send me away, then," she blurted, crossly.

"Let us not be too hasty. Your notes indicate that your episodes were almost daily before you came here."

"So what. You've cured me with all your stupid tests... And, anyway, the food's disgusting!"

The housekeeper bridled. "Roxanne Battie! How dare you? How can you be so rude to the man who has taken you in under his own roof?"

"Easily," protested Roxanne. "He don't care for me one little bit, do you, Professor? All you want is to find out about the fifth. Well, I'm glad I don't flip no more. I'm glad for me and, if that don't suit, well, I'm glad you ain't getting your findings. You can stuff your experiments!"

"Go to your room, young hussy!" stormed Mrs Brean. "That's more than enough. I will deal with you later!"

"You can't keep me here!" yelled Roxanne over her shoulder as she retreated.

That evening was a bad one. Roxanne refused Nadia's company. She felt so trapped. If only she could flip. If she could just get into the fifth she would stay there – despite the horrible grey world that it was.

Nadia was billeted on the floor above Roxanne. At around two in the morning, she was woken by the sound of a window breaking. The night staff came up the stairs and entered Roxanne's room. The shouting was awful.

Nadia got up and opened her door in time to see Roxanne clattering down the stairs with the two night staff in pursuit. Reaching the hallway, the girl continued down the connecting corridor that led to the dining room. Nadia followed and noticed blood on the stairs leading from Rox's room. She stopped. What should she do? The night staff would not welcome her presence. But her indecision lasted only a moment and she followed the blood trail down the corridor. Rox might need her.

She caught up with the night staff outside the dining room trying to open the door. Somehow Roxanne had managed to lock it or barricade herself in. The women took no notice of Nadia standing watching.

Then she heard a car draw up to the front door and in came Professor Williams. He had clearly been sent for and hadn't been far away. Rushing past Nadia, he joined the women pushing at the door and it began to open. Roxanne had pulled up a line of tables against it and they were taking some moving. Nadia was worried. Rox was hurt – there was blood – and the only way out of the dining room was through a second door kept locked at night which led to the laboratories.

As soon as the gap was wide enough, the professor squeezed himself through. The women were far too large to follow him. Nadia heard him remonstrating with Rox – she had not got away then. Nadia didn't hesitate. She didn't know what the professor would do but she knew he was angry; if she were there it might be better for Rox. The night staff blocked the doorway and wouldn't let Nadia pass but eventually she managed to shove the women aside and slid her slim form through the gap and onto the table that was jamming the door.

The first thing Nadia saw was the professor standing stock still staring at the wall; there were drips of blood on the skirting board. The key to the laboratories was in his hand which Nadia noticed was also red with blood. What was the prof up to? What had he done with Rox? She was nowhere to be seen; the door to the laboratories was firmly closed. Had he locked her inside?

The professor turned to see Nadia.

"Where's Rox?" she demanded.

"Er... she's, er... decided to leave..." the professor replied. Then he gathered himself together. "She wasn't happy here. You know that. Best she should go."

"Where?"

"We'll decide that in the morning. Now, I think you ought to be in bed, young lady."

The professor moved the table that was keeping the night staff at bay and directed that Nadia should be taken immediately back to her room.

"And Roxanne?" one of the women asked. "She was up to it again."

"I know," murmured the professor. "It's all in hand. She's chosen to go home. Leave that with me."

☆ ☆ ☆

The day after the incident in the dining room Nadia asked where Roxanne was. Mrs Brean was evasive; she said she'd no idea – Roxanne had simply left. Then Mrs Brean showed real annoyance and Nadia had to back off.

"Look here, young madam," she blustered, her face going the colour of a plum, "Roxanne has left the clinic – at least for the present – so I don't want to hear you mention her again. Understood?"

"Yeah."

"Right, you must have some study to do. Go and do it."

Nadia couldn't make out whether Mrs Brean was annoyed with Roxanne or with her for asking the question. It was probably a bit of both. Roxanne had left all her things in her room. It was odd - very odd. But she knew Rox had her issues. She wasn't the easiest of people to live with - Roxanne had problems that were not just about flipping into the 5D, as she taught Nadia to call it.

After Roxanne's departure, Nadia felt totally isolated but the professor tried to be nice to her and told her there were bound to be other new residents soon.

6

Tom got out of bed, stretched and searched for his T-shirt and jeans which must be somewhere in his bedroom amidst the scattered clothing, empty mugs, crisp packets and the remains of his rejected pages from his attempt at an essay for Swanney (Ms Swanson, English and history teacher). Truth to tell, studying wasn't something that commanded his enthusiasm. Like his father, who had been a fisherman, Tom believed he was destined for the sea. He was a natural sailor.

Living in West Bay now that summer was on its way was awesome. It was a bit of a drag in the winter when, to get to the local academy, Tom had to take two buses or walk three miles inland. But when the sun shone, his mates all came to him along with the streams of tourists in search of sea, sand and somewhere to spend their money among the harbour shops and cafés.

He was in Year 10 which meant he had one more year after his current one to attend school. He was almost as old as his dad had been when he had begun working full-time on the fishing boats. Since that tragic storm, when his dad and everyone aboard the *Merry Lynch* had failed to come home, Tom's mother had been struggling to find enough to keep them living at the Bay. Tom wanted to do his bit – but not even his father would have ever been contented with a living selling ice creams. In some ways, dying at sea had been a more fitting, if untimely, end for him than eking out a living on shore now that it had become almost impossible to make one from fishing. But, in the last few weeks, Tom had crewed for a rich yacht owner who had berthed his vessel up the coast. Tom Green was getting known. Perhaps – just possibly – one day someone would invite him to crew on a round-the-world yacht race. That was his dream. He had studied the racing craft that occasionally came into the mariner at Weymouth. When he had a bit more experience he would contact some of their owners. Yachts were for the rich but if you got to know the right people, opportunities might just open up.

That day, however, Tom was not expected on board a yacht. He had arranged to meet his mates and just hang out around the Bay and do whatever they found to do when people left them to their own devices.

Tom walked out of his front door and made his way to the harbourside. It was early. He didn't expect the others for an hour or so but he needed to get out. He spotted a yacht tied up at the end of the pier and went to take a look. She was stunning. Wow! It was not usual to see such a yacht actually in the harbour at the Bay but the water was particularly high that morning; she would have to leave before the tide turned. Tom spotted the signs of the crew preparing to cast off. He hurried along beside the harbour wall towards it; he did not want to miss this.

Then, suddenly, the sea seemed to rise up on his right and the harbour wall flipped around. The sun, which was still low in the morning sky, spun above him and Tom stared at his distorted feet wobbling against a background of flashing colours and violent sound - a cacophony of discords - then all was grey, flat and silent, and the world disappeared.

7

Alice was trying to keep calm. She did not want to expend any energy in her excitement but it was difficult. She had to pinch herself to check that this wasn't a dream; for the first time, she really was about to run for her county. Dressed in her vest of blue and white with the West Yorkshire county crest bearing a white rose on her right shoulder, she jogged onto the tartan track, did a few warm-up stretches and bounced on her toes. This was it!

Along the length of the finishing straight a stand full of noisy supporters were all shouting their encouragement. She knew her parents were there as well as some of her teachers but she deliberately kept her back to the stand as she identified her 400 metres start line in lane three. 400 metres was Alice's speciality. At fifteen, many of her friends had given up on serious sport but Alice had become dedicated to being fast and worked hard. She put from her mind the previous occasions when she had crossed the line first; today all these girls were new to her and she did not know how she would compare with them. All she knew was that they were the best in her age group of seven other counties in the north-east.

Concentrate, Alice told herself, get in "the zone". Great, she felt the zone coming on – all she could hear was the starter calling them to take their marks.

She settled in the blocks.

"Set..." Bang!

Alice sprang forward, quickly catching the girl in lane four and with no one on her left elbow. She rounded the bend feeling good. Down the back straight, she caught the girls in lanes five and six. This could be ... just could be ... her race... then, whoa! The track before her skewed to the right, she saw the sun pitching downwards to her left and the trees at the end of the back straight become a thrashing sea of distorted shapes and colours. Sounds slurred and became distant. Alice glimpsed her own feet zoom past her nose and her hands seemed to buckle. She wanted to scream but all power had left her. She couldn't breathe. She couldn't think.

8

Christopher James Francis Hengrove-Blunt was studying the form of the horses at the Wincanton races. He had no intention of gambling, of course – as a Year 10 boarder at Wincanton College he was under-age in any case. Any dabbling in such activity could get him expelled. And he was also fully aware that gambling could become an addiction that could destroy a person. He had no intention of ever betting for real; that would have spoiled the fun. For him it wasn't about winning money but outwitting the bookies who rigged things in their favour. For Christopher, it was the mathematical probabilities that intrigued him. He took into account not only the going, the handicaps and the horses' forms but the distance they had travelled, the experience of the jockeys and their compatibility to a particular mount, the trainers' record at Wincanton, the time of year, and whether the owner was going to be present and as much other data as he could muster. He factored it all in and gave each horse a probability rating. When it didn't work, he would examine the race in detail to discover what he hadn't taken into account ready for the next meet. Christopher enjoyed maths.

With a name as long as his, he had been known by his nickname, Hen, from the beginning of prep school; at the college he was officially known as Christopher but none of his fellow students called him that. He didn't care for his nickname because it didn't meet with his ambitions to be a respected establishment figure one day but there was nothing he could do about it. Hen's father was a civil engineer in Abu Dhabi and, ever since Hen was eight, he had been travelling to England to attend boarding school. He wasn't the only one in his class with parents abroad - many of the students came from distant places.

Anyone who didn't know him would have thought that he was older than he actually was. In some ways, Hen had missed the child stage.

Wincanton College had particularly suited Hen and he had done well. He was already studying the form at Cambridge to decide which college he should apply for. Should he apply for the same college as his father, or should he strike out at somewhere a bit different? And what subject should he take? He knew his parents would want him to do something that led to a profession - like engineering - but Hen couldn't resist the thought of taking on the challenge of pure maths. The thing was that he was rather introverted - he couldn't see himself on some building project in the desert like his father.

Hen was fascinated by the work of the code breakers of Bletchley Park and he secretly considered a career at GCHQ in Cheltenham – but that was an ambition known only to him. Although he was only fifteen, Hen was already lined up to sit for the GCSE maths paper. In the mocks, he was to tackle the most demanding maths paper his school could procure.

It was while he was sitting his mocks that Hen had flipped into the fifth dimension for the first time. The exam hall had disappeared in favour of a drab grey place with a plane inclined at approximately forty-five degrees to the horizontal. Everything had the appearance of being only in two dimensions. Black ellipses had passed along the slope and had given the impression that the whole plane was passing him by. Then, down to the left had been a tiny vortex – the only thing that contained anything that resembled colour. The longer he had looked at it, the bigger it grew and then, there he had been, back in the classroom on the floor with his fellow students looking down at him.

9

Donald Padget lit up a cigar - although smoking was prohibited in the clinic - and leaned back in one of Professor William's soft armchairs. He had turned up at the Winterford Clinic unannounced as he usually did - he liked to see people like the professor squirm. He spoke with a loud smirking American drawl which he used for his patsies.

"Look, Williams, I'm a busy man. I'm not here in London only because I'm on the board of Texman Pharmaceuticals that keeps you in business or to chair our European section of Tobacco Plus Incorporated, or even to promote my interest in Fox Defence Industries. In short, I'm here to tell you that I'm going to pull the plug on you and the Winterford Clinic - unless you produce something by the end of next month."

"Next month! But that's impossible. My research is progressing well - we're on the brink of a breakthrough and I've already begun my paper - but the scientific community doesn't work like that."

"Like what?" drawled the entrepreneur.

"Results in one month—"

"You've had three years!"

"And they have revealed a great deal. We need at least another year—"

"But you haven't got another year, Williams."

There was a tap on the door.

"Come," called the professor trying to look calm, and glad of the interruption. It was Mrs Brean, the housekeeper.

"I saw you arrive Mr Padget. Would you like some tea?" she asked.

"Tea? I'll take a whiskey," demanded the visitor.

"Oh dear," signed Mrs Brean, confusion added to her fear. "I don't think we have whiskey on the premises... We have teenage—"

"My filing cabinet, Mrs Brean. Bottom drawer," said the professor, in a resigned voice.

"Oh dear," said Mrs Brean again, as she pulled out a squat bottle of scotch and a glass from among a collection of other bottles.

The entrepreneur relaxed and smiled. "Single malt. You wicked man!" he chortled, taking the bottle from Mrs Brean and pouring himself a large tot into the only glass. "Now as I was saying—"

The director looked up to Mrs Brean and then the door. She took the hint and left, pulling the door tightly shut.

"It can't be done in a month," protested the director. "Even if I were to finish the paper today, it would take *at least* six weeks to get it published in a scientific journal—"

"I'm not interested in scientific journals," drawled the American. "How long before we get the results? That's all I care about."

The professor had always been fearful of losing his financial backing but, now, Padget was really putting the wind up him. His hands began to shake and he stammered, "I... I... I can do it in six months so long as—"

"So long as?"

"So long as I can dissect a brain – a brain of someone who has flipped into the fifth dimension. The thing is..." he paused to adopt an academic tone with authority, "I need actual physical evidence for the scientific community to accept my findings. The scans can only go so far. I need to observe and identify the actual physiological brain cells – the cells that are engaged when a person flips."

"And where are you going to get such a brain, Williams?"

"That is the problem. My team and others are convinced that there are a lot of young people who are dying as a result of fifth dimension traumas, but it's hard to say – impossible to say – that that's what killed them if they are not already known to us. There has to be concrete evidence of regular documented fifth dimension flipping or my findings will not be accepted. Scientists are notoriously rigorous when it comes to other scientists' claims. And, to make things worse, the coroners in my country and yours are finding all sorts of other reasons why these young people died."

"So how can you be sure that they *didn't* die of these other things?" asked Padget, waving his cigar in the air, scattering ash.

"Some will have done, but among them, there would be many who have expired in the fifth dimension." The professor thought he was getting through and some of his confidence returned.

"Which the world doesn't yet acknowledge exists. Not until you tell them," said Padget.

"Quite," the professor breathed. Had he won his case? "So you see my dilemma."

"Yet you have here," smiled Padget, with a hint of sarcasm, "among your patients, a kid who has definitely got this thing. I believe she is an in-patient."

"We don't call Nadia Simpson a patient – she's not ill–"

"Whatever you want to call this Nadia, Williams, is your business. The fact is you have your evidence here, under your own roof!"

"Yes, but she is a survivor and very unlikely to die. If she were going to die, she would have done it before she got here," explained the professor.

"Just suppose she did. Then you'd have your brain, wouldn't you? A perfect brain for the occasion."

"Yes, most definitely. But that is highly unlikely. Fourteen-year-olds in perfect health don't just die." Professor Williams felt sweat beneath his collar; he didn't like the way this was going. *Surely not...*

"Shame," breathed Padget in a resigned tone. The professor relaxed. "Such a pity you can't dissect her brain... But that's *your* problem, Willie boy," Padget added as if dismissing the thought.

"OK, Williams." Padget tossed the rest of his whiskey down his throat. "You've got until October or I shall foreclose on this place. Your project will be finished and this rather nice building will be mine, and you will be history... Get yourself a brain, Professor..." He pronounced 'professor' with a sneer. "Get yourself a brain, cut it up, and write your paper. I don't care about your so-called scientific community. October... I'll be generous, the beginning of November. How does that sound?"

10

Alice was angry. Anger had followed the shock, the frustration at being taken from the stadium, and the indignity of having to submit to a physical examination. But what made her really angry was the suggestion that she had taken something. Once investigated, an athlete could never remove the suspicion that they were a drugs cheat. Even when all the indications were negative, there would always be those who believed otherwise. When Dr Merlow had asked her if she had taken anything to "enhance her performance" - she had not been very tactful - Alice had just exploded. But then the world had become fuzzy again and it frightened her. She became calmer as she heard herself declare emphatically, "I'm no cheat!"

The doctor apologised. "I did not mean to infer you were... I merely asked the question. I have to. I have your answer."

Alice relaxed as she heard her father's voice calmly explaining to the doctor that Alice had been extremely disappointed when she had heard that athletics had been so badly let down by the state-sponsored drugs scandals that had blighted the sport she so loved.

"OK. But a young fit girl like you, Alice, doesn't pass out without an explanation. I want you to promise me that if anything like this happens again, you will come back in for some more extensive tests."

"Of course she will," Alice's father was saying. "If this happens again, her mother and I will be very worried... but it's probably a one-off," he added.

Alice remained quiet. She was aware she had almost suffered some kind of flip right in front of everybody when she had got angry just then. She was still angry, but fear was uppermost and the feeling of flipping subsided. *What if I have got something really wrong with me?* She was thinking as the doctor looked her in the eye, and said.

"I don't believe you're a cheat – but I do want you to be honest with me if this happens again."

"OK. Yeah, OK," Alice agreed. "Now, can I go home?"

"Most certainly. Take it easy and eat something."

Alice got carefully to her feet and held her chin up to appear to look normal. Thankfully, by the time she had reached the door, she *felt* normal. She turned to Dr Merlow. "Sorry," she said. "It's just... drugs are so wrong."

"Glad to hear it," said the doctor.

☆☆☆

Within a week Alice was feeling herself again and was back in training. She was also looking forward to a disco night at the school. It was the last big fling of the term and everyone was expected to dress up. Alice had got a beautiful crimson and pink dress that made her feel a million dollars; it had belonged to one of her cousins – but it fitted her well and hadn't needed much altering. She checked on her accessories, a hairslide and matching handbag that sparkled with diamonds – fake diamonds, but great-looking all the same. But far from fake was a gold charm bracelet that her parents had given her for her fifteenth birthday. It was the most valuable thing Alice had ever owned.

On the afternoon of the disco, Alice had her hair done by an expensive hairdresser in the centre of the city. By the time her friend, Becky, and Becky's twin brother, Zac, arrived in their father's car to drive them to the school, Alice was feeling pretty good. You could see that Zac was impressed. The effort had been worth it. Becky looked fab in blue satin with her long blonde hair piled up on her head. Alice was glad she had kept hers down and gathered in the hairslide, so it didn't look like she was trying to copy her friend.

Cameras and mobiles clicked and recorded the scene as the members of year ten arrived in all their finery. Intriguingly, some of the staff had made a great effort, too, and it was interesting to see some of the things they were wearing. Dr

Oakland, the headteacher, was there looking very dapper. It was his last term. Alice would miss him. He was a head who cared about each student and, by the time they had got to the end of year seven, knew all their names by heart. He also knew all of their individual potentials – even better than they did themselves.

It was, however, Miss Brown, a young teacher of modern languages, who was attracting everyone's attention, fascinating the boys with a low-cut dress and sparkly stuff in her hair. She had also attracted the attention of Mr Ramsbottom, the PE teacher, who Alice and Becky quickly decided was Miss Brown's intended target.

Becky pulled Zac's arm and told him to take his eyes off Miss Brown. Zac blushed – he hadn't realised his bewitchment had been so noticeable. He tried to think of something witty to say but his brain had gone into numb mode.

"Zac," begged Becky, "for goodness sake ask Alice to dance."

"Er... er... of course," said Zac, giving Alice a genuine smile. "Sorry, the occasion just got to me."

"Something did," laughed Becky.

The next dance was lively with a strong beat. This was great. It was too early in the evening for the contact sort but that would, no doubt, come later. The two friends put down their soft drinks and made their way to the centre of the hall and joined the dancers. Zac wasn't a bad dancer - if a bit enthusiastic. But Alice was unusually good and Zac was delighted to be standing up with her as his partner. He didn't doubt Alice would be dancing most of the evening.

The beat of the second dance was heavy and hard. It grew in intensity as the dance progressed and Alice kept in time with it. Then it happened. The dance floor went soft and crumpled. The stage and the other dancers spun and blended into a streak of mixed colour. The beat became a jumble of sound and then distant.

Alice came to with her back against the wall. She was on the floor and covered in Coke from someone's glass which was still rolling on the floor beside her. Zac was bending over her with a horrified look on his face. People were crowding around. Alice felt sick. She must get up; this was crazy. Then the head was there and Mr Ramsbottom was demanding: "Give her air!" Alice tried to get up but her heels were far too high to allow it. She kicked them off and then her foot slipped in the Coke and she fell back down again.

"She's drunk," stated an unsavoury boy who Alice and her mates were glad was leaving the school.

"No, she's not," argued Becky. "Not unless you have put something into her drink."

"Me?" he said, all innocence. It was not that he wasn't morally up to it but just not capable of organising it. Becky relaxed.

But Alice was crying. It had happened again. What was wrong with her? Was this going to happen every time she was having a cool time? She knew no one had put anything into her drink. Apart from a bruise on her backside, Alice felt completely all right. She had suffered a severe loss of dignity but, more than anything, she was angry and frustrated.

The PE teacher had already dialled 999 and as she was heading for the bathroom with Becky to clean herself up, she was surrounded by paramedics. No amount of protestations were going to persuade them to leave her alone.

"Look, Alice," said Becky. "They can't just leave you; it's in their contract. You can discharge yourself at the hospital."

"I know what I have to do," sighed Alice. *I promised the consultant*, she thought, *I know I can't ignore it.* She allowed herself to be led to the ambulance. Then she told Becky and Zac who had followed her out to go back inside and enjoy themselves.

"Apologise to people for causing a scene and spoiling the fun," she added. She waved them away and turned to the paramedics. One of them was carrying a glass – her glass with what remained of her drink in it. They were taking it with them to get it tested. First, drugs to improve her performance, and now the recreational sort. She was livid.

"I HAVE NOT TAKEN ANYTHING," she yelled. "Why

won't people believe me? I'M NOT A DRUGGY!" Fired up with anger, Alice dodged out from the back of the ambulance and ran around it. The ground heaved, the ambulance smeared into a spiral of yellow, green and red tail lights and Alice knew it was all happening again but she was so angry that she didn't care. The experience went on and on. Black balls were floating beside her and she stared at them. She had left the ambulance smear behind and the cacophony of sounds that came from the street had faded and been replaced by an external silence that seemed to allow her brain to make its own noise as it seethed with anger. At last, Alice calmed down and took her eyes off the spheres and was transfixed by the vortex just in front of her to her left. Then she saw her feet slip through it.

11

Alice became aware that she was sitting in a flowerbed in the dark park opposite the school. Her landing had not been violent. She got to her feet and saw not only the ambulance but also a police car and loads of uniformed figures milling around amidst dozens of students and teachers. She guessed what had happened – she had vanished and they were looking for her. Her head was clear and there was nothing physically wrong with her; there was no way she was going back there and facing all those people. Alice knocked bits of soil and vegetation from her now ruined outfit, took off her gold bracelet and pushed it into her bra. Then she walked across the park and down to the hospital. Alice did not go into A&E but the main entrance where she calmly approached a reception desk and asked to see Dr Merlow.

As she waited in a corridor near Dr Merlow's room, she texted Becky:

"Am OK. At hospital. :) Al. x "

Then she rang her mum and dad.

☆☆☆

"I am pleased you acted so sensibly," Dr Merlow said, as she put away her stethoscope. "I was ninety-nine per cent sure what you suffered on the running track was not going to be a one-off."

Juliette Merlow was dressed in evening wear too. When she heard that Alice had presented at the LGI, she came straight in. She did not want to allow her to go through the gamut of tests the A&E doctors would almost certainly have prescribed. Dr Juliette, as she told Alice to call her, thought she knew what had happened to Alice. Although it hadn't hit the headlines yet, it was a growing phenomenon among young people. Judging from what had happened at Alice's school, it was not going to be ignored by the media much longer. That was another reason she had not hesitated to break her date – it was essential to get Alice safe from them.

"You know what's up with me?" asked Alice.

"Yes. I am pretty sure that if I run every test available, you would come through one hundred per cent fit. There is nothing physically or mentally wrong with you. And I am certain that when they test your drink, all they will find is lemonade."

"Coke."

"Coke, then... In one way you are a very fortunate girl, in another not so lucky."

"I don't get you."

"I'll explain. You'll need to listen to this carefully." Alice nodded. She was listening. "You might have grown up learning that there are four dimensions - three dimensions of space, left-right, forward-back, up-down, and one dimension of time."

"Yeah," agreed Alice, "we live in a 3D world and travel through time from past to future."

"For most people, that's all that matters," continued Dr Juliette, "but scientists have long suspected a fifth dimension - and even up to ten of space and one of time. The other dimensions are sort of 'inside' - for want of a better word - the four main ones."

"Like Russian dolls?"

"That'll do... I see you are an intelligent girl. All ways of trying to describe the other dimensions are bound to be metaphorical - we don't have the words or the experience. Not until now, that is..."

"You're not saying I am entering into some kind of fifth dimension?"

"That's exactly what I am saying."

"How come?"

"We don't know that. And, before you ask, neither do we know why a few do - an increasing few - and the vast majority of us don't. But the sad thing - and this is why you're a lucky person - is that we suspect that some people who

48

enter the fifth dimension do not come back alive. And, again, we do not know what determines who survives and who doesn't."

"Some people come back dead?!" exclaimed Alice. "How do you know that they died of... of flipping into a fifth dimension, and not of other things?"

"Because ... because there are signs, patterns that, as a doctor, you get to recognise. But the problem is I can't prove it. There are no clinical indications – like I said, in every physical or psychological test you would prove completely healthy. The deaths all appear like unfortunate accidents, but I and a few other doctors think we have detected a pattern. And some come back in different places, which could only be explained by what you call flipping. A few, like you, remain alive and unblemished by the experience and can talk about it; and what you are describing is completely consistent with what others say. You used the word 'flipping', for example; it's amazing that you did that when you have not heard anyone else use the word."

"It just felt like that."

"Precisely."

"The difficult thing..." Dr Juliette's tone changed and became solemn. "The difficult thing you will have to accept is that if it has happened twice, it will almost certainly happen again. And, as yet, we do not know any way of preventing it. It will always be dangerous for you ... so far you have been lucky."

Alice sat silently. She had had little idea what lay ahead of her in her life except that, if she did well enough at her GCSEs, she would stay on at school and do A-levels. And, of course, there were her ambitions on the track. But now...

"I want to go home... talk to Mum and Dad," she said.

"I anticipated that. They are on their way. In fact, officially, I shouldn't have shared this with you until they had arrived but you're a sensible person and I think you will all be able to handle this better if you had some of your questions answered straight away... Have you any other questions?"

"It makes sense. A lot of sense," said Alice, thoughtfully. "In fact ... Dr Juliette, have you experienced the fifth dimension, yourself?"

"No. Only through my patients ... Do you trust me?"

"I... think so. It's all so... confusing, and I wish... but can you help me? I mean... is there anything that can be done for people with this?"

"Maybe. There is a lot we do not know about the phenomenon, but the more people we find, the more we can work on some way of helping you... and you could help other people through being involved in the research... Your parents should be here any minute. They are bringing you some everyday clothes – if you want to change. You have a lovely dress, but it's got a bit battered. As soon as they arrive you can change and go and get something to eat Then we can all come back here and I'll talk to you all together."

Alice was surprised to discover she was hungry. Her mum and dad were pleased to see her eating so heartily. It confirmed what she was telling them – she was not sick. And this time the shock had been nowhere near as bad. Now she kind of knew what to expect, and Dr Juliette had told her she hadn't got something wrong with her – not in the normal way. She explained about the fifth dimension.

They listened without comprehension. But Alice was putting a brave face on it. "That's my girl. I'm so proud of you."

Just then Dr Juliette came over to their table. "Can I join you here? Save you coming up to my office."

"No problem. Are you sure? We're holding you up," said Alice's dad as he saw Dr Juliette still in her evening dress.

"Oh. Don't worry. He'll wait. It's only just around the corner. Now, has Alice explained?"

"Yes," said her mother. "Something about an extra dimension. I don't understand. It's so... out of the ordinary."

"That's a good way of putting it." Dr Juliette explained her theories to Alice's parents. She answered as many questions as she could but when her father became exasperated and said, "Next year is Alice's GCSE year. What about her future?" Dr Juliette put on a professional face.

"I have a proposal. I have been in touch with a professor at the London School of Medicine – the Post-Puberty Research Department. She has told me about a clinic in London that is researching the phenomenon and they are looking to recruit young people with this condition to their programme. It would be a live-in situation... It is fully funded."

London? All Alice could think was, *That's way down south!* Lost in some minor panic somewhere inside, Alice heard her father saying they would have to think about it.

They parted without saying anything much. It was a lot to take in. All that Alice could think as she dragged herself to her bedroom was: *What an evening!*

In the quiet of her room, she became aware of her phone buzzing. A text from Becky:

"You OK? Where r u?"

The text had been sent several hours earlier.

"At home," she wrote, "back from hospital. Am OK."

The phone buzzed an instant reply:

"Gr8. We had a massive search looking for u. Then ur message came u were OK."

Alice returned:

"Sorry. Ruined ur evening. Tell Zac sorry 2"

"Z's OK. Danced with Ms Brown. It was a hoot. C u 2mor?"

"K. Where?"

"At yours. 10 am?"

"Fine. Nite."

"Nite."

Alice turned her phone off. The silence was golden. She knew she was on her way to live in London – without her mum and dad or brother! She had no real alternative. It would be most definitely the scariest thing she'd ever done.

12

The Winterford Clinic was a large detached building in leafy grounds. Built between the world wars in a quiet backstreet, it boasted three floors and a mock Georgian façade. Nowhere in central London can you get away from the sound of traffic but this place was as quiet as you could get. Alice looked up into the wide blue spring sky with its line of aeroplanes heading for Heathrow and listened to the birdsong from a clump of trees at the end of a well-kept flowerbed. It was not like their semi-detached house in West Yorkshire at all; it was like nowhere she had ever seen before and it looked so outrageously posh. It had a weathered stone engraving on the gate post that said, "The Hattersley Foundation for Sick Children" but the polished brass plaque beside it simply bore the title "The Winterford Clinic".

Alice did not feel sick, nor did she consider herself a child and bulked at the inscribed words, but her father said that the name was probably only historical, dating from the twentieth century. He also pointed out that Alice *had* got a condition that needed sorting out and that, until she was eighteen, she was technically still a child.

"Very technically," Alice protested. "You can get married at sixteen. That's only a few months away." She'd turned fifteen the previous autumn.

"You can. Do you feel like getting married then?" said her mother.

Alice pouted - until she recalled that pouting was a thing children did. "Course not," she said, brusquely. She had never had or wanted a boyfriend. She had kissed a boy once - technically, she claimed - at a party, but that was it. Her father said that she should be grateful that she qualified for the care on offer - even if it meant admitting she was still a minor.

Mr Downey paid off the taxi and joined his wife and daughter as they stood in front of the high ornate gate. "This place would be worth a bit," he declared. "Professor Williams' foundation is not without its supporters." They were not having to contribute anything to Alice's treatment or her keep.

Mr Downey pressed the rectangular button below a silver keypad beside the gate. A squeaky voice came from the device. "Yes?" Mr Downey replied. "Mr and Mrs Downey with Alice. We are expected." There was a click and the large gates began to open slowly by themselves. Alice felt as though she was entering some kind of computer controlled alien world.

Alice carried a day bag over her shoulder and her father manhandled a large heavy suitcase across the gravel - the stones were too loose to drag the case on its rollers. Her mother held a basket of stuff for a picnic if it was needed. As they climbed the semicircular flight of steps, a cheery woman in a pink uniform dress greeted them.

Inside the heavy oak front door, the hallway was all polished dark wood – wooden floor, wooden panelled walls and a wooden staircase with thick balusters supporting a wide shiny bannister rail, which would have been tempting to slide down if it weren't for the ornately carved newel post with which it terminated. The brochure had said the place had been built as a private family home in the 1930s but Alice couldn't imagine anyone wanting to live in such a place. She thought it was ugly.

The pink-uniformed lady led them into a large room on the left. It was evidently the director, Professor Williams', study. Books of all ages lined the walls – most of them with medical titles. A large mahogany desk with a dark-green leather top stood at an angle across a bay window with leaded panes. She showed the three of them into three armchairs arranged around an ornate coloured marble fireplace. The grate was obscured by an embroidered fire screen.

"Please make yourselves comfortable," said the cheery woman. "Professor Williams will be with you shortly. Can I get you some tea?"

"Thank you, that would be nice," answered Alice's mother.

Alice cringed. She hated it when her mother put on her posh voice. What was wrong with sounding "Leeds"? Alice kept quiet. As far as she was concerned if they didn't like Yorkshire here, they could stuff it. She was beginning to feel in charge of herself again.

The woman left with the same smile. Perhaps, if the truth were known, she was from some foreign place, too. People came to London from all over the world, didn't they?

Professor Williams turned out to be a small man in his late forties with a goatee beard and pointed ears. When she saw him, Alice immediately thought, *elf*. He had not taken the big leather chair behind the desk that Alice assumed he would but brought up a chair and joined them around the hearth. He was clearly not from the south of England either. It turned out he was from the Scottish borders and had trained in Edinburgh. He asked them about their journey.

By train the journey had not been difficult, Mr Downey explained. They would not have to stay in London that night – not unless Alice needed them.

"Alice will be well looked after here," Professor Williams assured them and, turning to his new subject, spoke kindly. "When you have finished your tea, Mrs Brean will show you to your room. We have put you in a double room that overlooks the back of the house, but there will only be you in it, Alice. I'm sure you'll like it. Have you any questions for me?"

Mr and Mrs Downey wanted to know about the treatment and when it would begin. They were told that Alice would be introduced to the house regime and the tests would begin the following week. The important thing, for now, was to meet the other residents - he didn't call them patients. Alice asked about the Internet. Was there a connection in her room? What about Wi-Fi? No, there weren't connections in the bedrooms but there was a computer lounge on the ground floor that the residents could use. They didn't allow residents access to Wi-Fi in their bedrooms because it was essential they concentrated on the clinic regime.

"You will understand that when people are vulnerable to 5D attacks, it is vital that we allow them a proper sleep pattern. Unfortunately, sometimes we have to protect them from the outside," explained the professor, "but be assured, Miss Downey - can I call you Alice?" Alice nodded, reluctantly. "Be assured that the computer lounge is available by day for your use."

Alice was not assured. She was used to contacting her friends day and night. Occasionally they snap-chatted late into the small hours. Her friend Becky would be expecting a call right now. But it was OK because her parents had bought a mobile package with high data usage. She had already checked there was a good signal - she had texted Becky from the taxi. So Alice smiled and Professor Williams seemed satisfied. Mrs Brean, a rather stern looking woman in a dark-green uniform, appeared as the cheery pink lady cleared away the tea things and Professor Williams handed them over to the housekeeper to see that Alice was installed in her room.

Then, all too suddenly, Alice was on her own in a large draughty first-floor bedroom with a view across a croquet lawn. She snap-chatted Becky a picture and began to unpack. Ten minutes later her parents rang her to see if she was OK.

"I'm fine, Mum. Get the early train," she said, as confidently as she could. "Ring me when you get home."

13

A bell rang somewhere and Alice heard footsteps along the corridor. Was it a call for a meal? She felt hungry. She took courage and ventured out. She thought of the pictures of baby birds fledging. Like them, she was sort of growing up and leaving the nest. As she left her room she almost collided with a skinny girl about her own age.

"Hi," Alice squeaked. She didn't mean it to be a squeak – it just came out like that.

"Hi," answered the girl. "You must be Alice. They said you'd be moving into Roxanne's room."

"Roxanne?"

"Yeah. Left a couple of weeks ago... You a 5D?"

"5D?"

"Yeah – 5D survivor."

"Yes."

"Same with me. I'm Nadia. I've been here coming up for a month."

"Old hand."

"I'll show you the dining room. It's where we eat lunch and tea which they call dinner here. We have breakfast in the 'breakfast room'. It's posh here. You from the north?"

"Leeds."

"I'm from Bristol. Come and get some lunch – or dinner or whatever you call it – and meet the others."

They proceeded down a flight of stairs and along a passage to the back of the house. Twenty or so people were gathered around tables. On the side, healthy-looking salad-type food was set out for them to help themselves to. Alice didn't mind salad. She had anticipated that in a clinic you didn't eat burgers and chips so much. Actually, she was glad; she couldn't have coped with chips all the time. Nadia led her to a table where two lads were sitting.

"Meet our other newbies," she said. "Tom arrived yesterday and Chris two days ago."

"Hi," said Tom holding out his hand.

"Hello," said Hen. "Not Chris. Call me Christopher." He spoke with a rather plummy accent that Alice thought he must be putting on. She had never heard anyone actually speak like that for real.

"We can't call you Christopher. It's too long," protested Nadia. "Bet your friends don't call you that. What's your nickname?"

The young man coloured a little before saying he didn't have a nickname. Then his phone bleeped a text.

"Make the most of that," said Nadia. "They'll stop you bringing that out of the computer room before long."

"It's a phone. I don't need Wi-Fi," said Hen.

"Makes no difference. No communications outside of the computer room. It's part of the 'regime'."

"Sounds like a prison!" exclaimed Alice, panicking.

"It is... sort of," answered Nadia. "But don't worry, you'll soon learn how to get around things." She leaned over Hen's shoulder as he read his text.

"Girlfriend?"

"No, school chum."

Nadia read: "Hi Hen. How's it going? Sorry you're having to miss the horse trials. Keep in touch. Arch—"

"Hey. That's rude," said Hen, piqued. "I'm not surprised they've taken away your phone." But Nadia was laughing.

"Hen?" said Nadia. He said nothing. "So that's your nickname. Hen. I like it." Hen blushed crimson. "How did you get that? Are you chicken or something?"

"It comes from my name," said Hen, reluctantly.

"Go on, then, tell us your proper name – your full name."

Hen sat up straight wearing an expression of defiance. "If you must know, it's Christopher James Frances Hengrove-Blunt. I come from a very old family."

Nadia exploded. "Keep on like that and I'll flip for sure,"

she chortled.

Tom came to Hen's defence. "Lay off the man. A fellow can't help his name."

"Yeah," said Alice, who was wondering when it would be her turn to be laughed at.

"OK," smiled Nadia. "OK. I guess that was, like, a bit harsh... But if your school *chums* - she emphasised the word - call you Hen, then the rest of us can."

"Well," said Hen, stiffly, "if you must."

Alice felt for him. "If you don't want—"

"No. It's OK," he smiled. "But thanks..."

Alice soon learned that Tom was feeling much the same as she was about being in London. He explained that this was the first time he had been anywhere much; he couldn't ever remember going to bed without the sound of the sea in his ears.

"You'll get used to it," said Nadia. "It gets more, like, normal after a couple of weeks."

"I've lived away from home ever since I was eight," explained Hen. "But I do miss school. It has become home. I miss the friends I have grown up with. I've been at Wincanton College since I was thirteen and many of them were at the same prep school as me. It's not what I would want to do. I mean, being here right now. The others are all making their sixth-form choices."

"Already?" said Alice, astonished. She was still only coming to terms with her GCSE choices – A-levels were far off.

"Yes. It's all rather keen at my school. I'd even begun asking myself about whether I should aim for Cambridge like my parents and my brother. They want me to do engineering but I was thinking, well, that I might do something different and that would affect my subject choices at A-level... but all that... well, it's on hold now, isn't it? Being here has changed all that."

"Until the doctor at the hospital said that I wasn't the first to use the word 'flip'," said Alice. "I thought that what was happening to me was, like, just me... But, Nadia, did I hear you calling it 'flipping', too?"

"Yeah. But *I* don't flip – the world does!"

"Exactly!" exclaimed Alice. That was precisely the right way of putting it.

"Same for me," said Tom. "*Inside* – you know what I mean – it's a strange place, though."

"Yes," agreed Hen. "Grey with a kind of slope?"

They all nodded.

"What is it?" asked Alice. "I mean, what exactly is it? Is it really a different dimension?"

"I think the question should be: Where is it?" suggested

Hen. "I don't think it's just happening inside my head. It's like I'm in *it*, not *it* in me. And that would certainly be the case if it is a true fifth dimension beyond time and space."

"They *call* it 'the fifth'," said Nadia, "but they still think it's inside our heads... At least Prof W does."

"Prof W?" queried Tom.

"Professor Williams," explained Nadia. "You can't go 'Professor Williams' all the time, can you?"

"Guess, not," Hen smiled. "Everyone gets a nickname then?"

"Only if it's long and posh."

"Right," said Hen, still smiling.

"So apart from flipping, the only thing we've got in common is that we're all in year ten," said Alice.

"Pretty much," agreed Hen. "And British."

Coming from Hen with his upper-class accent, Alice thought she'd take that as a compliment. She had not tried to change her accent here as her mother had downstairs. Tom had a distinctive soft Dorset burr and Nadia, a wide-mouthed Bristol twang.

"I don't care for this thing about confiscating phones," said Alice. "You can't take someone's phone off them."

"Well, as long as you surrender *one*, you can stash a second, I guess," suggested Nadia.

"Is that what you've done?" wondered Alice. "Is that what you meant by getting around things?"

"Nah. I just didn't admit to having a phone. I'm poor, ain't I?"

"Being poor doesn't stop people having phones," said Tom.

"Yeah, I know. But Prof W don't know that, do 'ee? He don't get teenagers."

"But he knows I've got a phone," said Alice. "Mum told him."

"And he's seen mine," said Hen.

"And that green woman knows about mine, too," added Tom.

"Old Brean," nodded Nadia. "Then you're stuffed,"

"So we're all stuffed," said Alice with a sigh. "We could use yours, Nadia," she smiled.

"Nah. I ain't saying I've got one. I just said the prof didn't take one off me."

"Oh. Right," said Alice, doubtfully. She didn't press the question.

66

14

If the fifth dimension was a true reality, it would have been a world-shattering find. But few people apart from a few professionals and the 5D survivors themselves were aware of its power. No one appeared interested except for Professor Williams and a few others in his field. He believed it was centred in a particular part of the brain but he also believed that there was an actual reality beyond – the explanations of his subjects agreed in detail about what the fifth was like. And none of them showed any other symptoms; they all appeared to be in perfect health. In fact, so perfectly normal that he had not yet found the neurological trigger. It was all rather frustrating but with three new subjects, he was sure he would find it soon. It was just a matter of time – time he did not have much of – nevertheless, he was sure he was almost there.

Prof W was in no doubt that the episodes from which his subjects suffered were anything other than 5D experiences and he saw it as his job to research them. Kaluza and Klein – early post-Einsteinian physicists – had independently concluded the existence of a fifth dimension as long ago as the 1920s. Now, a century later, the majority of particle physicists accepted string-theory, which required may be as many as ten space dimensions and one time dimension as the basis of reality. Kaluza and Klein had believed the additional dimensions were curled up inside atoms - a trillionth the size of an atom - and were responsible for the electromagnetic force. But now, it seemed, evidence of a new kind of extra dimension was emerging - one that could exist well beyond the quantum level and replace the traditional Einsteinian understanding of space-time. And the remarkable thing about this new development was that some human beings could actually experience it and live to tell the tale. Professor Williams had been captivated by the idea of the fifth dimension... and the possibility of being the first to bring it to the world as a proven theory. The thoughts of receiving the accolades of an amazed world - even winning science's highest award, the Nobel Prize - pervaded his dreams.

Prof W was not alone in acknowledging the phenomenon - scientists across the Western world were aware of it - but the only one besides himself engaged in research into the phenomenon was a Professor Bradford in the United States with whom the British Research Council expected him to consult. He and Professor Bradford did not get on however - Bradford had a completely different approach - and Williams was more than happy to work alone and take the entire credit.

Hen's college had explained away his episodes as some

rare kind of epilepsy. They assured parents that it wasn't catching. And the idea of a fifth dimension was so incomprehensible – something that belonged only to the world of geeky scientists – that the sensationalist press overlooked it; their readers did not want to read about the hair-brained stuff that weird professors were coming up with. Supersymmetry, decoherence and M-theory had not sold newspapers in the past, and neither would some idea about a fifth dimension. If it didn't contain at least a hint of scandal or a direct threat to the reader, popular newspapers weren't interested – especially if it took some effort to get your head around it.

Prof W liked it that way. He wanted to keep the world away from his clinic – and his subjects away from the world – until he was ready to show his hand. But with young people in a networking generation, this was proving very difficult. He had quickly learned, however, that to sever them from their communication devices was like cutting out part of what made them human. For the current generation, the five human senses were augmented by the smartphone. But the fear of being sent home without a cure, added to the camaraderie that existed between what the clinic called "the residents", enabled him, to some degree, to get away with it. He hoped that the provision of a state of the art computer suite that could be accessed at the prescribed times was just sufficient to keep their frustrations in check.

On the afternoon of their first full day, Alice, Tom and Hen were invited into Prof W's study. Nadia called it his den. The professor was full of smiles.

"Now that you, Alice, Thomas and Christopher have settled in," he began, "it is time to induct you into the regime we offer at the Winterford." *Offer,* thought Alice, *does that mean we have a choice?* But Prof W quickly confirmed that the only choice they had was to stay or leave; Alice recalled Nadia talking about Roxanne *escaping.* The professor told them that they would have to deposit their smartphones in a locked drawer in the computer lounge. Each drawer was wired to enable the phones to be charged. They were later to discover that the drawers were also electronically locked and opened only at the times predetermined by the professor.

"I need your one hundred per cent commitment and concentration on the tasks to ensure the tests give true readings," explained the professor.

"What kind of tests?" asked Hen.

"I'm coming to that," said Prof W, gently. "The first involves regular detailed brain scanning using the latest MRI and scintigram techniques. I will explain in more detail before each test. The rest of your bodies will be explored using all the most up-to-date imaging technology, your body fluids will be constantly monitored and biopsies will be taken and tested in the lab."

"Biopsies?" queried Alice.

"Tissue samples... Don't worry," smiled Prof W, "we only use minute samples. Tiny needles - you won't feel anything. For the most part, we use swabs."

Alice felt embarrassed. It was as if they were going to be specimens rather than people. This professor was creepy.

Hen, however, was saying, "I understand why you have to do this, professor. But what are you going to do to cure us of the 5D flipping?"

"That will depend on what we find out from you. You and countless others will benefit from your being here."

"What about exercise?" asked Tom. "We can't be cooped up here. I and Alice were quite active before we came."

"Don't worry about that, Tom. The regime includes constant exercise. We need you to do it prior to the tests. We monitor how much you are getting and what type, as we do your food intake."

Alice had a sudden desire to go home. Why had she ever consented to come? She'd hadn't felt a bit like she was going to flip ever since she had agreed to leave home for this clinic. She felt her insides go cold. She could leave - leave right now. All she needed to do was get her things and take a taxi back to King's Cross station. Her father had said there was a train to Leeds at least once an hour. She looked at Tom and Hen. Hen seemed to be cool, but Tom looked terrified. She had no idea what Tom had got to do to get home, except he had said it had taken him far longer to get to London than it had taken her. He had said that West Bay had no railway station - well, not one with a railway line since Dr Beeching. And anyway, she knew he had no money. His mother could not afford to give him one hundred pounds "just in case" as her parents had. For a fleeting second, it crossed her mind that she could take him to Leeds, but it was in the opposite direction from his home and what would his mother say to her son running off to the north of England with some strange girl? Besides he would never consent to it - apart from anything else, Leeds was a long way from the sea. No. He would stay here as Nadia had.

Something in the way Nadia had said it made her think she was disappointed Roxanne had bowed out. What did she say? Something like she couldn't hack it. She was counting on her staying. So was Tom. He said it wasn't working in West Bay, and if she was honest with herself it hadn't been working for her either. Then, lastly, Alice knew that to go home so soon would not please her parents. They were proud of her; they believed she was made of sterner stuff. No. No, she would have to stay. At least with the other three, she wasn't alone.

"Alice. Alice." The professor was calling her back from her reverie. "Are you with us?"

"Oh. Yeah. Sorry."

"5D?"

"N... No. Not at all. Just thinking of my parents... They haven't texted that they are home yet."

"That's an example of why it is important to forgo these phones," smiled Prof W. "As soon as you have communicated, you must tell them you will be incommunicado except for an hour a day."

"Incommunicado?"

"Offline," translated Hen.

"Oh. Yeah," mumbled Alice. *Only one hour a day!*

"Any more questions?" asked the professor.

No one spoke.

"You may leave. You are free this afternoon to explore the house and grounds but please don't enter the technical area or the laboratory. These are out-of-bounds unless you are undergoing tests. I do not need to say that you must not leave the premises. Access to the front of the house," he indicated the gardens and gravel drive they could see through the window, "is for the staff only."

"Thank you, sir," said Hen. "We are fortunate to have such facilities."

"You're welcome, Christopher. You play croquet?"

"Yes, sir."

"Alice, Tom?"

They both shook their heads.

"Perhaps Christopher will teach you. Now off you go and enjoy this fine afternoon... Oh, and I will need you to deposit your electronic devices in your locker drawers by five o'clock."

"Thank you, sir," said Hen again.

They left the room and Tom immediately said to Hen, What's with all this 'yes, sir, no, sir' stuff? You sucking up to him?"

"Not exactly," said Hen. "Just making him think I'm on his side."

"What does that mean?" asked Alice.

"He could be up to something and, if so, it does to keep in with him. If someone trusts you, they are more likely to be open and off their guard."

"How do you mean?" asked Alice.

"It's beholden on us to trust no one from the establishment we don't know. My parents can't vouch for Reginald Williams."

"Sounds, scary," said Tom. "You should write novels."

"That would be a possibility, except I much prefer mathematics."

"Are you saying you think there is something wrong with Professor Williams?" persisted Alice.

"He doesn't figure all that much on the recognised scientific websites. He's too mysterious. I am suspicious that all is not quite as it seems. We're guinea-pigs, right? But to what end? It may just be he wants to get a professional accolade but whatever it is, I have this feeling it's all about *him* and he's not really interested in *us* except as subjects for his experiments."

Alice was shocked. She had felt Prof W was a bit creepy, but she hadn't thought of him being caught up in anything sinister.

"All I'm saying," added Hen, "is that, at this stage, it's better not to give too much away, not until we see what is truly happening."

"Right," said Alice, "but with all the testing, he'll know more about us than our parents do."

"More about us than we know ourselves," grumbled Tom.

"But none of his machines can tell him what we're thinking and if we can let him believe we are meekly complying ..." said Hen.

"Yeah. I get it," said Tom. "I like the sound of it. Suck up to him and keep a bit back."

Alice went out into the garden feeling a lot happier. She didn't want to walk out on these people. They were all in it together ... and they were all 5D survivors, so, for now, this is where she belonged.

That evening, in the draughty sitting room with its chintz curtains and a small TV in the corner, Hen told Alice that in the few days before his arrival, he had studied all he could find on extra dimensions. He had discovered and read up on the Kaluza-Klein stuff as well as some of the more controversial theories including the latest ideas surrounding the subject. He was amazed at just how little there was. A search of "fifth dimension" didn't throw up much science. There was plenty of hippy stuff – a pop group singing about the age of Aquarius and a Vegan tattoo parlour in London's East End, a leisure centre in Gloucestershire and luxury British chocolates. But Hen believed he had experienced more than five dimensions; he believed he was already into the sixth space dimension and a time-warp.

15

Alice and Tom hit it off from the start. Neither of them had lived away from home before and, remarkably, they discovered they had been born on the same day, the first of October – Alice in Leeds and Tom in Dorchester. But, beyond occasional family trips to Scarborough, Alice knew nothing of the sea. She was fascinated by Tom's stories.

"You're very lucky living in West Bay," she said.

"I know I am. It's a bit cut off from other stuff though. Most of the young people go off to uni or get apprenticeships elsewhere and they don't come back. Everyone is old, well, almost everyone. Three-quarters of the people that live around us are retired off-comers, and most have no real understanding of the sea. There're only two kids in our year that actually live in West Bay – the rest kind of rock up on a weekend. You never know who's going to be there."

"Is there a running track?" Alice thought the place sounded intriguing – much more attractive than her city.

"You wanna laugh? I guess you've got to go to Exeter or Yeovil, even Bournemouth for that. It would take, literally, hours on the bus, if there is one and you can afford it. One kid in our year – she was brilliant, really fast – her parents had to drive her to Yeovil twice a week and sometimes to events all over the South West. She used to train on the beach and cliff top paths. If you can run on the shingle and up and down East Cliff, you can run anywhere, I guess."

"What sort of distances does she run?"

"Don't know. They moved away in the end; Bristol, I think."

"Because of her? Because she needed to have a place to run?" Alice asked, wondering how much *her* parents would sacrifice for *her*.

"Don't know. I didn't know her that well. Boys and girls keep a bit separate... They would be brilliant parents if they did, though. My mum would never contemplate living anywhere else. West Bay's the only place she would ever want to live. It would kill her to move."

"What about you, Tom?" asked Alice. "Would you ever move?"

"You've got to if you want to get on. If I got a job sailing... But that's all finished now, isn't it? no one's going to take on someone that's likely to freak out any time. The first time it happened I ended up in the sea, and I was only walking down the quayside!"

"Don't say freak out, Tom. It's not!" protested Alice.

"You're right. But that's what people say," he grimaced. He told Alice all about the first time he flipped and the times

78

afterwards – both in school and on the bus.

"Life just became unbearable until eventually, Mum consented to let me come to London," he concluded.

"So now you are here, what are you going to do?" asked Alice.

"Hang around until they find a cure, I guess. I'm going to be sent homework from school... but sport's out of the question unless this place organises something... How does anyone stay fit?"

Alice sat up straight with her hands on her knees. "I dream of trips to a gym or a swimming pool... And you know what I'd really love?"

Tom guressed. "A state-of-the-art running track...? And some fast runners to compete with?"

"Bingo. You're cool. You get it... That Mrs Brean doesn't, though. They have everything in London, don't they? Do you think, if we said...?"

"You gonna ask? Alice, you're a brave one."

"Maybe... Not yet... Let's see what happens."

16

Hen was showing Tom the finer points of croquet. Alice found it complicated and dull and it took her ages to get her ball through the first hoop. Nadia wasn't interested at all. Tom persisted; he didn't get Hen's explanatory physics – angles and forces and things – but he did find he had a feel for it.

Alice and Nadia sat on a bench under a magnolia tree beside the lawn and chatted. They didn't know it was a magnolia tree until Tom told them. He knew so much about the natural world.

"You had many flips, Nadia?" asked Alice.

"Not many but enough. One was right in front of the doc at the hospital. He told my dad I had to come here. I didn't have much choice or them dreaded social workers would come round and I'd be packed off to some foster family. Anyway, I had to do som'ut, didn't I? It was getting, like, stupid. The good thing is, well, sort of, Dad's picked up this new girlfriend. She's as bad as he is for the drink but she can do stuff for him. She didn't when I was there of course, but she don't starve and I knew she wouldn't let him starve... So I didn't argue."

Alice summoned up a bit of courage and asked, "Nadia, what exactly happened? When you flipped ..."

"Do you really want to know?"

"Yeah, Nadia. Until I came here it was all about me. But here it isn't."

"Sure, I'll tell you. Look, Alice, I'm glad you're here. Don't get me wrong, I'm not glad that anyone else suffers from this flipping thing but you do and the world ain't so lonely... You ain't going to run away, are you?"

"Like Roxanne?"

"Roxanne was different. She had her problems."

"So what happened to you, Nadia?"

"I were on the Downs – there weren't nothing I had to do that afternoon. I like the Downs. They're wide and open and green. The only houses you can see are posh ones far away."

"That's in Bristol?"

"Yeah. The Clifton Downs. You been?"

"No. All I know about Bristol is that there's an old suspension bridge – the first one or something."

"Yeah. You're in the right place. That bridge goes across the Avon Gorge near the Downs. It was a nice day and I didn't want to go home early. Up there on the Downs it was real sunny. There was a couple of football matches going on and I watched for a bit then I crossed the road to the edge of the gorge. From where I were standing you can see the bridge if you lean out a bit. I was happy. It's important that you believe that, Alice."

"I do Nadia. Why shouldn't I believe you?"

"Loads of people wouldn't."

"I do. Go on, Nadia."

"I leaned against the fence and thought about the wildflowers you can see in the summer. There's all sorts and colours. I guess they like it there cause no one's allowed to go beyond the fence; it's a sheer cliff. The river's a long way down."

"You like wildflowers?"

"Yeah. They do their thing like they want – nobody planted them there. But I weren't thinking just about the flowers... I were thinking... but... but I can't tell you that."

"Go on, Nadia, it's OK."

"Nah. You ain't ready to hear it... and I ain't ready to tell you."

"Nadia, you don't have to tell but–"

"Nah. You're OK. I reckon you don't tell people some things when you've only just met them."

"I guess not... but the things you were thinking then, Nadia, on the Downs – is it them that got you in here?"

"No. Look. I'll tell you that inside stuff some day but not

today..."

"Fine," Alice forced a smile. "So—"

Just then Hen's red croquet ball scooted across the lawn towards them and Alice had to lift her foot as it shot under the bench.

"Watch it!" she shouted.

"Sorry," called Hen coming across to rescue his ball. "Tom's getting too good at this."

"It can't be in the game to fire your ball off the grass," laughed Alice.

"No," said Hen, "But it is quite in your interest to do that to your opponent's ball. That was Tom's shot – an effective croquet."

"Sounds like a war!" exclaimed Nadia.

"Well, I suppose it is a bit. Only no one gets hurt," chuckled Tom.

"Except for innocent people who happen to be in the way," joked Nadia.

"Exactly like a war, then," said Alice.

Hen scooped out his ball and placed it on the edge of the lawn and the game continued around a hoop on the far side.

"Anyway, do you want to hear the end of my story, Alice?" asked Nadia

"Yeah. Sure."

"Well, right there on the Downs, I flipped," Nadia told Alice all about what happened in the hospital and how it eventually ended in her coming to the Winterford.

Alice listened, engrossed. "I've never met anyone like you, Nadia. You're clever."

"Clever! That's something I ain't! If you think that, you got things to learn, girl."

"No. I don't mean, like, school work and stuff, I mean wise. You've got things sorted. I don't have to think about my meals and how to spend money and how my dad's coping. Mum and Dad have got it all covered. I just, well, do as I'm told... mostly."

"Nobody tells me what to do – not if I can help it. Anyway, Dad don't know what time of day it is some of the time. It's easy in here. Like a holiday in a posh hotel – not that I've ever stayed in a posh hotel."

"I guess... Look, Nadia, I've got parents who love me. They fuss too much but I'd never think of leaving home. They've given me a hundred pounds in cash just in case I want to take off and go home any time... But, I promise, I'm not going away. Not like Roxanne. I promise."

"Thanks. If you hang around long enough I might tell you about what I was thinking... I mean, that day on the Downs... If you want to hear it."

"Yeah. I do. When you're ready."

"In this place, I reckon you'll grow up fast. You won't want to do just what you're told." Nadia smiled.

Alice laughed. "It's already happening. That Prof W's a creep and I'm not going to do all that he says."

17

At his luxury home in Arlington, Virginia, Donald Padget sipped his bourbon with the air of a discriminating drinker. On his desk was the picture of his eldest daughter wearing a daisy chain that she had made some years before when they had first visited Scotland and bought a castle. He glanced at it and smiled – things were coming together nicely.

In his office across the Potomac in Washington DC with a view of the Capitol, Padget was a respected entrepreneur with an international property portfolio and on the board of Fox Defense Industries and Tobacco Plus Inc. But the businessman secretly harboured grander ambitions that included the White House itself, and much, much more. On his wall was a big picture of a daisy chain – this time without his daughter.

Leaving the lift, Padget approached his PA. He propped his portly frame on her desk and bent his sandy-coloured head rather too close to her and half whispered, "I need a flight to London, Sophie, say the day after tomorrow."

Leaning back, Sophie smiled. "Yes, sir. First class return?" He didn't like her pulling away from him and felt peeved.

"Yeah," he drawled. "Give me two nights. Book me a suite

in the Dorchester."

"Park Lane?"

"Yes, Sophie. Park Lane," he said sarcastically. The truth was he couldn't fault his PA on her efficiency - but she was strictly business and had made it quite clear that his advances were unwelcome. Padget didn't like being told no. As soon as he could do it without causing too much of a fuss he would replace her with someone who wore a daisy somewhere.

18

Ugh! Alice made a face as she swallowed yet another mouthful of revolting stuff for the x-ray machine to track. "How much more of this?" she complained.

"No talking now," said a dragon of a nurse. Alice decided the woman must be an alien from some dull planet in some remote galaxy – she displayed no human emotion. Or perhaps she was a machine – a robot nurse. Alice had never seen her smile or express the least drop of sympathy. Alice felt like telling her where to go but gave in and lay on the machine bed as instructed. *If I don't*, she thought, *that freak will tie me down*. Alice was learning when and how to be defiant. Now wasn't the time. She lay obediently under the machine but it seemed she still had to be tied down and have clamps positioned against the sides of her head to stop her moving. As the nurse leaned over to fasten the restraints, a pretty gold pendant in the shape of a daisy flower slipped from under her collar. It seemed incongruous – too delicate for a dragon.

Alice couldn't help smiling. "That's pretty," she said. "I like daisies – kind of summery."

The nurse forced the pendant back inside her uniform and

barked, "You've no idea, have you?"

"No idea about what?" asked Alice.

"I've already told you," the dragon's eyes bore into her, "to be silent!" And she pulled the final strap painfully tight with a jerk. Alice winced.

What was all that about? Alice wondered. *She didn't seem to like me seeing her pendant. No robot then – pure dragon.*

Alice closed her eyes and pretended to drift off. The jabs didn't make her as sleepy as the nurses thought but she guessed they were meant to and the nurses would only increase the dosage until they took effect, so she fooled them. Alice reflected on how devious she had become and, in particular, how prone she now was to lie. *Mum and Dad would be horrified if they knew how dishonest I am,* she thought.

The testing was turning out to be much worse than the teenagers had been led to believe. They had to produce urine samples three times a day, get weighed-in every morning before breakfast, and record all their calorie intake on a card they were forced to carry around with them on a ribbon around their necks, together with a monitor on their arm that would record any trip they should make into the 5D. They weren't allowed to take them off – even in the shower. Well, officially, but Alice did take hers off. No one said anything, which was a relief because she would have hated to learn she was being spied on in the bathroom.

"It's not just being constantly prodded, poked and having needles stuck into me throughout the day," Alice complained to Nadia, "it's that it makes me feel, well, somehow different from the person I thought I was. Every morning I wonder what nauseating and uncomfortable tests I am going to have to stomach. It's weird being wired up to all the machines. It kind of makes you wonder what they know about me that I don't." And she shuddered at the thought that Prof W could make all her data instantly available on some kind of world-wide information web – information that would be meaningless to her. "In fact, I'm not sure if I know who I am any more," she sighed.

Alice's dignity was challenged but it was Tom she was worried about. She really felt for him. None of this was in the least bit compatible with a free spirit like his – he would have far fewer problems with the isolation on a solo round-the-world yacht race than in the clinic. The loneliness he experienced when trapped in this environment was painful to watch. He was sort of shrinking. How long could he stand it? She, Tom and Hen had now been in the clinic for nearly a month.

Before she came, Alice had been led to believe they would be allowed home for a weekend after four weeks but it didn't turn out that way. Prof W said nothing about any time away and when Alice asked him he seemed surprised. He answered that he would consider her request if things progressed well. She was angry and for the first time since coming to the Winterford felt like she might flip, but the sensation soon went away.

19

That same afternoon a ginormous bee or perhaps some other stinging insect flew into Alice's room. She was supposed to be doing some school work but this animal began exploring every corner, and Alice leapt to her feet. She opened the door but it wasn't interested in going out that way. Finally, it made a beeline for the window but collided with the glass. Alice decided she must open it fully. It was one of those windows that slid up and down rather than swing out.

Keeping an eye and ear open for the whereabouts of the bee-thing, she tugged at the hooks on the bottom of the window and pulled it up. It remained in place for a couple of seconds, then there was an enormous thump somewhere to the side followed by the window crashing down. Glass shattered and sharp panes fell in all directions both inside and outside. Alice screamed in shock.

Staff reacted and came running up the stairs.

Nadia felt a surge of panic. She burst out of her room above. The sound of a window breaking reminded her of Roxanne. After all, it was the same room! The boys reacted, too.

Alice was in tears. "I didn't do anything," she sobbed. "I

only opened it to let a bee-thing out." In all the confusion the bee-thing had vanished – probably through the broken window, totally freaked out, too.

The staff were not at all sympathetic. It was Nadia who asked. "Are you OK, Alice?"

"Yes... No... I don't know. Why did it do that – the window?"

Hen examined it. "Broken sash cord," he pronounced, pointing to a rope dangling from the window frame. The weight will have fallen in its box. He tapped the side where Alice had heard the thump. "It was an accident waiting to happen because it was supported by only one cord. There should be two but someone hasn't bothered to repair the one on the right. Look, it's been painted over."

"Are you cut anywhere, Alice?" asked Tom, genuine concern in his voice. Alice felt better just having these people around her; having their friendship was great.

"I'm OK," she said softly."Loads of glass but no blood."

Later, Alice found herself in Nadia's room for the night. The window wouldn't be repaired until the next day and Alice said she didn't mind sleeping on Nadia's floor. She didn't want to be alone and it felt like a sleep-over.

As the settled down to sleep, Alice murmured, "I need to get out of here! I haven't had a flip since I left home. I'm not sick but what *is* going to make me ill is being cooped up in this place.

"You're not going to leave are you?" Nadia spoke with a waver in her voice.

"No. I promised. Straight up! As long as you stay, I'll stay. But I don't know how you put up with it. You've been here the longest... It's kind of become your home, hasn't it, Nadia?"

"Yeah. I know it's not nice being tested all the time, but it's better here than I get at home. I get breakfast, lunch and tea every day, don't I?"

"Nadia, have you ever been allowed home since you've been here?"

"Never asked."

"Don't you miss your family?"

"There's only my dad, in't there? And it's best I keep away. Social Services have got involved now. When I was there I told them we was managing and as long as I turned up at school they left us alone, but that's all changed, innit?"

"I thought your dad had found a girlfriend?" Alice put a hand over her mouth. "Sorry, I don't mean to pry."

"That's OK. It ain't private... Yeah. But she got into a fight and the police have carted her off. Now it's just the social worker. If I went home now, they would cart *me* off, too. When I'm sixteen things will change but that ain't until next year. It's better for me here. In this place, I'm the same as the rest of you."

Alice grappled with the implications of what Nadia was saying. Having a loving family whom you couldn't ignore restricted your freedom but being on your own as a minor reduced your options even further. She'd never thought of it like that before. "So while you're in here you're safe and your dad's happy?"

"Well, happy ain't really the right word. But, yeah."

"So what will you do when you've finished... finished here?"

Nadia shrugged. "No idea."

"I had plans and dreams..." began Alice, pondering on what might have been.

"That's not what it's like where I come from. It's about surviving each day," explained Nadia. "You daren't think about tomorrow. If you do - and take your eyes off today - you might not get to tomorrow. You have to watch for your opportunities... I did think, once, I would have liked to work with children but that's all over now, ain't it? That door's shut because of the flipping. They wouldn't have me."

"So you see this clinic as your place of opportunity?" Alice was getting it.

Nadia smiled. "Course. With you and Tom and Hen, it's quite cool really. I'm actually doing more learning, too. Hen's a good teacher."

"You *never* feel trapped here?" Alice thought there might at least be a little bit of frustration.

"Nah. I could walk out of here and no one could stop me. But I'd be a fool."

"I'm not going anywhere, Nadia, but I do need to get out of this prison. I need proper exercise. I need to run."

"Look, if you want to go outside for a bit... like for a run, I can organise that. But you'd have to have someone go with you – you never know what you might meet after dark around here."

"How?" wondered Alice, intrigued. "And why after dark?"

"Well, you couldn't exactly go out in the daytime, could you?" laughed Nadia. "You'd be missed. No, the best time would be after everyone except the night staff have gone home."

"But it's all locked up," protested Alice. "There're hedges all around the gardens and the front doors—"

"Open with a code," said Nadia with aplomb. "So do the gates. In the dark, you wouldn't be seen."

"I guess you know the code, then. How?"

Nadia smiled and nodded. "All you have to do is watch. It was the first thing I did. If you sit on the landing you can see which numbers Old Brean uses ... I did that so that I knew I

96

could escape if I needed to."

"So," pondered Alice, "if I waited until after Mrs Brean and the kitchen staff have gone home—"

"You will only have the night staff to dodge... But you mustn't go on your own."

"I know. Will you come?" asked Alice.

"Nah," dismissed Nadia. "Too risky. If I get caught they might send me home and then it'll be a foster home or some other institution for sure... Besides, I can't run like you; I'd only slow you up."

Alice was set on the idea. "I'll ask Tom. I know he's pining to get some fresh air. Perhaps Hen will come, too."

Nadia chuckled. "I can cause a diversion. Pretend to have a bad flip; that'll bring them up to the second floor... If they catch you, you won't let on that it was me that told you the code?"

"Course not. I'll say I found out the same way you did."

20

The following day over breakfast, Alice caught Tom deep in thought – his eyes had a vacant expression. She wondered what he was thinking.

"Tom, do you want to go out for a run?"

"A run? Out?" He looked up startled from his reverie. "Outside?"

"Yeah. Outside. Keep your voice down. Around the streets. There's no seaside, but you can run as fast as you want... I've got a plan. I know how we can get out – Nadia knows the door code." Alice outlined the strategy.

"Cool! But... what if we get caught?"

"Tom, the worst they can do is send us home. And my parents would approve I reckon. They would go mental if they thought I was being punished as well as being subjected to all the testing..."

"I can't afford to go home, Alice. I've got no money. And Mum would be angry and make me get a job in the supermarket... and I will still have these attacks of flipping that'll restrict what I can do."

"No," said Alice, decisively. "I've been thinking about this.

Prof W's *not* going to send us home – he needs us to experiment on. He's not going to let us go. That's why he's keeping us from going anywhere for the weekend and stuff – he's frightened that we might not come back."

Tom mulled it over and then came to a decision. "OK. I'll do it. I've got to do something or I'll die of boredom. So when? And where would we go?"

"Just around the streets. We'll remember which way we went so we can come back the same way. And we can go any night you like."

"What about Hen and Nadia?" wondered Tom.

"Nadia doesn't want to go," explained Alice. "I've already asked her. In any case, she would be necessary to create the diversion – take the night staff up onto the second floor. You think we should ask Hen?"

"Three people are better than two," thought Tom. "I don't know what London streets are like; he will."

Alice was doubtful. "Can we trust him? All his sucking up to Prof W makes me uncomfortable."

"Yes, I trust him. And we've got to ask him; it wouldn't be fair to leave him out. I will put it to him," said Tom.

"OK. Fine. I'm really up for this," Alice breathed a loud sigh. "Anything to get me out of here for an hour."

Tom approached Hen and put Alice's plan to him but he wasn't game. He was too nervous. He was afraid of being caught.

"It's too risky. It's not worth it," he said, slowly.

"But what can they do to us?" protested Alice.

"That's not the point. It's against the rules. My parents wouldn't approve."

"Neither would mine. But they'd understand," protested Alice. Hen looked away; he was clearly not ready for it. Alice turned to Tom. "OK," she said, "so it's you and me, Tom. You still up for it? I need to get out!"

"Yeah..." Tom hesitated. "Maybe, but Hen—"

"I need to get out!" Alice almost shouted. "Please!"

"OK," said Tom. "I get you Hen, I do. But *I* have to get out, too, or I'll go mad... They shouldn't keep us cooped up like this."

"Cool," said Alice, relieved. "Let's make it tomorrow night. As soon as it's dark."

They worked together on the details and the plot was finalised.

"What about our monitors?" asked Tom.

"Oh. Just... just take them off," Alice blustered. "We can't risk them showing we've been outside."

21

The following evening, Nadia gave the performance of her life. Hen kept to his room. Alice and Tom sneaked into the lobby and Alice keyed in the code. Click. She turned the lever and the door swung open. The cool evening air struck them and Alice thought she could fly. But they were only in the front garden – there was still the gate to open with another coded lock. Alice tried the same code again, but nothing happened. She tried once more. Nothing. Quite clearly it was a different code – probably one that allowed people into the drive that were not granted entrance to the house. Without more than a second glance, Alice began to scale the gate. It was three metres high but it was not topped with anything sharp. Tom hesitated, then followed without a sound. Alice slid her hands down the vertical railings as she lowered herself onto the pavement. She was safely outside. Outside! A thrill filled her heart as she saw Tom's feet hit the pavement, and then... Oh no!

Alice felt a surge of panic mixed with wonder as it overcame her. Why now? In all the time she had been in the clinic she hadn't come anywhere near flipping.

She couldn't prevent it. A huge wave overtook her and she hurtled into the fifth dimension. As soon as she arrived in the grey world she caught sight of Tom. In all the weeks they had spent together, he hadn't flipped either but here they both were in this same odd grey place. They could travel together!

Then Tom became aware of Alice's presence. Instinctively they reached out to each other as they slid towards the vortex. Then, just as suddenly as it had come on, they were out of the fifth dimension and sitting together, uninjured, on the pavement across the road from the clinic.

"Wow! We both went," grunted Alice. "Together."

"Yeah. First time for ages. Why'd it happen then?"

"It happens..." reflected Alice, as she stood up and knocked the dust off her jeans, "I reckon, it happens whenever I feel free - I mean, like, in the zone. The first time was when I was flying down the back straight and the second was when I was dancing and—"

"Excitement?"

"Yeah. Free and everything..."

"What're we going to do now?" asked Tom.

"You hurt?"

"No."

"Feel ill?"

"Quite the opposite," Tom declared.

"Right, we came out here to go for a run and I'm still up for it. What about you?"

"Yeah. Let's run! Which way?"

"End of the street." Alice pointed to the nearest corner. "Race you!" Her trainer would have been horrified at her sudden burst - she had quite forgotten all that he had instilled into her about warming up.

It was a tie. Alice was impressed with Tom's speed - he hadn't talked of any athletic ability. Brilliant. The sun was now setting but London was not dark at all. They turned left and Tom looked up. "No stars in this place, ever."

"Too much light pollution," suggested Alice.

"Too much pollution, full-stop."

They reached the next junction. "Which way now?" wondered Alice." We don't want to get lost."

"Right."

"OK. Let's make it right, then left, then right, and so on. Then we won't get lost."

At first, they jogged and then ran hard until they were out of breath. Eventually, a large road came into view with lines of noisy traffic; red buses, black cabs, white vans, and large shiny cars were all on a mission to get out of London, or perhaps into it. There was a line of shops, brightly lit with displays on the pavement covered with all kinds of things from clothing to fruit.

They came to a betting shop and an amusement arcade.

"There's one of those near where I live," panted Tom as they passed. "Mum calls it the den of iniquity."

"Why's that?"

"Legal robbery, she says. If I were to go into one of those and spend as much as a penny, she says she'd disown me."

The arcade was lined with bright, flashing machines making jolly sounds, and each one had a man or woman, boy or girl, standing in front of it feeding it coins. Most seemed to be men.

"What's the lure? A big win?" Alice had stopped to look. These were the first young people she had seen outside since she had arrived in London.

"Maybe. I don't know. They come down on holiday to West Bay and spend hours in a place that looks and sounds exactly like it does here in London. Weird."

They passed a launderette and then an off-licence, with a man in a turban serving his customers, before the shops ended and were replaced by the steps of a big dark church with high black wooden doors, firmly shut. It looked forbidding. They stopped jogging.

"What goes on here?" asked Alice.

"St Peter's Church of England, Wilburt Street, Diocese of London," read Tom. "It's a church."

"Looks scary."

"It's Victorian. They liked high imposing buildings. But it won't be Victorians inside it any more on a Sunday. Look, there's a picture of a rock band on that notice board. Cool. The church in West Bay's full of old people."

"That's it!" exclaimed Alice.

"That's what?" asked Tom.

"That's it. Prof W can't stop us asking to go to church, can he? I mean, freedom of religion and all that. He would *have* to let us out to go to church."

"You go to church at home?"

"Sometimes. Not very often. But Prof W doesn't need to know that," insisted Alice, intent on her next bid for freedom.

"I've got a bible," stated Tom.

"You go to church in West Bay?"

"You kidding! They're all over seventy. I watch them come out. No, Mum said you should always have a bible when you go on your own somewhere. It's some kind of family superstition. She said her gran would have insisted on it."

"Do you read it?"

"Never opened it."

"But, if you produced it, you could, kind of, prove you wanted to be let out on Sundays," suggested Alice.

"You're cunning, aren't you?"

"No!" protested Alice, instinctively. "Well, yes... I guess... But not really. I never thought of myself as being cunning... I'm just trapped... Truth is, I don't know what I am any more." Alice flung her arms against her sides and sighed.

"I know what you mean," said Tom "It's like, well here I am in a London street with a girl from the north with a different accent who's never seen my home or ever been on a boat. This shouldn't be me, but it is."

"Do you mind being with me?"

"Of course not! You're cool. You got us out. I wouldn't have done this without you... It's just, like, not what I ever thought I would be doing."

"You're like a duck out of water?"

"Like a sailor washed up miles from the sea..." Tom smiled. "I guess we'd better start heading back."

They retraced their steps back passed the dark church, the bright arcade and then left, right, left, right until they were back in the street with the clinic.

"Race you," shouted Alice. Tom chased on but was completely done in this time as he staggered up to the gate twenty metres behind Alice.

"You're fast!" he gasped. "My adrenaline's worn off."

Alice bounced. "Now I'm feeling much more like me. What about you?"

"A duck," he breathed. "No water, but I'll do. Better than I did on the inside."

"Good. Me too. Ready for the gate?"

"OK. You go first. Let me get my breath... And watch you don't slip half way up; it's beginning to rain."

Tom followed Alice, climbing as stealthily as he could while she waited for him on the inside, impatient to get out of the rain which was getting heavier. A light came on in Nadia's window above them. They looked up and saw her waving – she was ready for them. When they heard her begin to shout, Alice and Tom crunched up to the front door across the wet gravel. Alice keyed in the code. Footsteps sounded on the stairs and the night staff were shouting back at Nadia. Alice smiled. She waited until the noises were all from upstairs and then opened the door, silently.

They tiptoed up the stairs to Tom's room on the first floor without being noticed and stood and stared at one another. They were both still dripping; they laughed under their breath. What an adventure!

"We must do that again!" exclaimed Alice in a whisper.

"Yeah. I feel great," beamed Tom. "Here, grab this." He threw her a towel. They took off their wet trainers and Tom got two glasses of water to drink.

"That was ace. We *have to* do it again!" exclaimed Alice.

22

Ten minutes later, Nadia and Hen put their heads around the door and Tom ushered them in.

"How'd it go?" asked Nadia catching the mood.

"Great!" said Alice, excitement oozing from her glowing body. She felt more like the Alice of old. Then she noticed Tom all wet and felt gooey inside and her knees go wobbly. This wasn't like the fifth coming on but something else. *Whoops!* Alice thought to herself. If their eyes had met ... but Tom had his head down; he was avoiding looking at her. Had he sussed her thoughts, followed her gaze? Alice pulled herself back as she heard herself say, "We got right up onto a main road as far as a church. It gave me an idea. Do you think they would let us out to go to church on Sundays? They couldn't stop us, could they?"

"Wanting to go to church would sound odd after all these weeks," said Hen, casting a cloud on the proceedings.

"He's been grumpy all evening," laughed Nadia. "I told him to go to bed but he said he was worried about you."

"Nothing to worry about, mate," muttered Tom. "I'm not the kind of person that gets lost."

"It's quite an up-market district," added Alice. "Quite safe. no one gave us a second glance."

"You can't be sure of that." Hen was indeed negative.

"And guess what," laughed Alice. "I know I shouldn't be happy about it really but as soon as we got outside we both hit the fifth. And we were together inside."

"What! Together? You could see each other?" Hen was now really interested.

"It was the fresh air of freedom," said Tom. "I never lost sight of Alice. We met inside. Everything was the usual grey except Alice wasn't. She looked the same as outside."

"Interesting," said Hen. "So what did you do?"

"We joined hands and went through the whirlpool together and landed on the other side of the road," Alice explained.

"Then we decided to carry on with our run," said Tom.

"We weren't going to waste that... besides, I felt, like, great." Alice added.

"Are you going to tell Prof W you flipped?" asked Nadia.

"Course not! He'd ask too many questions. We left our monitors inside, didn't we? We couldn't risk them showing stuff that would raise suspicions."

"Inactivity would show up, too," said Hen. "That would look odd."

"So, I was asleep. I can't be responsible if the thing went

wrong!" Tom insisted.

"I'll tell them I accidentally dropped mine down the loo," said Alice. "Tell them I thought it was broken."

"You really are cunning," laughed Tom.

"Positively devious!" chuckled Nadia.

Alice coloured. Now she was plotting to be a bare-faced liar! Maybe she was going to be one of those teenagers that her father and mother talked about as "going off the rails."

"I hope you won't have to pay too heavily for this," said Hen. He really was in a mood. "I think it is time we got some sleep now."

"Oh. You grumpy thing. You're jealous! You could have come with us, you know," said Alice as lightly as she could. He had worried her but she wasn't going to admit it.

"I'm not so ill-advised," he answered. He got up and shuffled out of the door saying good-night as he went.

"Ill-advised?" queried Tom, after he had gone. "What's that supposed to mean?"

"Daft," translated Alice.

"But it *wasn't* daft. We got out and we got back and it was fun," protested Tom. "And thanks to you, Nadia. You were brilliant."

"You're welcome," giggled Nadia. "I... I might just join you next time ... maybe."

"We'll have to rely on Hen for the distraction then."

They laughed.

"I'd better be off, too," said Alice. "I'm ready for the best kip I've had in ages. Thanks, Tom."

"You're welcome."

23

Alice was still on a high as she weighed-in for breakfast after a wonderful sleep. She beamed at Tom conspiratorially as they tucked into their cereal. But the euphoria was short-lived. Prof W came into the refectory and barked: "Alice Downey, Thomas Green. My office please... now!"

Had they been spotted? Alice felt a mixture of anger, deflation and terror. Tom wore his sheepish depressed face. Had Prof W found out and, if so, what was he going to do about it?

Like naughty children, Alice and Tom followed Prof W as he strode briskly to his office. There was no chance of them exchanging anything but glances – no way of planning a plausible explanation.

Inside the office, Prof W took his chair behind the desk and directed the young people to two upright straight-backed chairs in front of it. Looking passed the head of the director, Alice could see the gate they had climbed and the road outside, where they had experienced an hour of freedom. Her mind traced the road to the church and the bright lights of the off-licence. Next time – if there would ever be a next time – she would continue going... Well, she might if it weren't for her promise to Nadia.

"So, what have you to say for yourselves?" the professor was demanding.

Alice's mind came back to the present. She was not going to admit to anything. Let the man be more specific in his accusations. Tom was dumb.

"I'm waiting."

"Something we have done?" asked Alice, wondering how she dared speak so boldly. But hearing herself, she became braver still.

"Do I have to spell it out? You have been told never to remove your monitors. We need to know every time you flip. I was beginning to think that you were never going to flip – either of you, despite your medical history. Now I hear you have removed your monitors and have been on an excursion into the fifth without reporting it. Did you ever intend to report it?"

No mention of an escape. They had removed their monitors before leaving but surely that was a lesser offence than sneaking passed a supposedly secure door and leaping a gate into the outside world. Alice looked at Tom. She hoped he would remain dumb and leave the talking to her.

"Sorry," she said. "We forgot about the monitors."

"Were you ever going to tell me about your flip? What do you have to say for yourself, Thomas?"

Tom continued to look down with a sheepish expression.

"May I remind you. You are here because we want to study your problem – not just for *your* sake but for the sake of everyone who may suffer from this in the future. This facility costs a lot of money to run. I need accurate and reliable data – and that means you behaving responsibly. Don't you think that the very activity which you have avoided reporting," the professor cleared his throat, "is highly significant for the study?"

What was the director on about?

"I... I don't get it," stammered Alice. The director had still not mentioned leaving the premises.

"YOU DON'T GET IT?" the exasperated professor sprang to his feet and moved to come around his desk, but then calmed himself, thought better of it and sat down again. He continued.

"My information is that you both went on a trip into the fifth – together – the first since you arrived here. Don't you think that what you were up to, *together*, was significant? Now, nobody here has encouraged such... relationships... but whatever their morality or otherwise, the outcome for us is highly significant. I'm not interested in the rights and wrongs – just the facts."

So that was it. Clearly, he had no idea they had been outside. And the way he kept saying "together" with a knowing nod and sly smile indicated that the man had decided they had been involved in some kind of romantic activity and it was that which had triggered the flipping.

One part of Alice wanted to disabuse him, but that would involve being asked what they were really doing. It was annoying to be accused of something completely untrue - and something her parents would be worried about - but, in here, in the prof's eyes, it was apparently not seen as so terrible. But how had he found out so quickly that they had had a 5D flip? It had happened outside the building and if any CCTV cameras or anything had picked them up there, the prof would know what they had really done. There were only two other people who knew - Nadia and Hen. Nadia would never have told.

"Who told you?" demanded Alice, belligerently.

"That is not important. What *is* important is for you to play the game while you are here. Now I want you both in the lab right now for extensive deep brain investigation. You should be pleased that I have managed to find out - your experience could provide us with a break-through."

Alice and Tom followed the director to the lab. Tom had still said nothing. His eyes were lowered; he looked neither at the professor nor at Alice. Alice wondered what he was thinking. What would his mum make of it all? She would probably be as shocked as hers.

The director called over a technician and began talking to her, leaving the young people on their own for the first time.

"He thinks we were... we were..." Tom tailed off, embarrassed.

"I know," whispered Alice. "Sorry."

"Are you going to tell them the truth?"

"No. Let the prof think what he likes."

"We know what caused the flipping," said Tom, "perhaps we should—"

Alice was defiant. "He's not going to find anything anyway... whatever we've done." She was adamant she was not going to admit to being outside because that could be the end of any further escapades. "And if he does think he's found something, we can put him right *then* and tell him what really caused it ... if we have to."

"The fresh air on the outside?"

"Freedom," said Alice, relishing the word.

"But if we don't say anything and everyone thinks we... My mum will kill me."

"No she won't, Tom. You're not in the habit of lying to her, are you? If they tell her that, she'll believe you when you tell her the prof got it all wrong. Let them think what they like. The alternative is being trapped in here forever."

"But these tests—"

"Will reveal nothing. What I want to know," spat Alice, "is who ratted on us?"

Prof W returned with a technician - a fake smile on his face. "Who's going first?" he smirked.

Alice stood up and looked the professor defiantly in the eye. Whatever they thought, she was going to maintain her dignity. She turned her pale blue eyes to Tom over her shoulder, conspiratorially, and gave him the thumbs up.

Tom admired her; you had to hand it to this girl. He returned the smile. He relaxed. Things could have turned out a lot worse. At least he was not on his own; they were going through this together. There was indeed a "getting together" but not the kind the professor thought.

24

After tea, the mystery of how Prof W had found out about the flipping was solved. Tom managed to corner Hen in his room and, rather clumsily, accused him of treachery.

"It could only be you. You and Nadia were the only ones to know that we had gone into the fifth. If it had been caught on camera anywhere, the prof would have known we were outside the gate when it happened... And Nadia would never have ratted on us."

"Your logic is perfect."

"What do you mean?"

"I mean you have correctly deduced how Professor Williams found out."

"You're admitting it?!"

"Yes."

"WHAT THE HELL DO YOU THINK YOU'RE PLAYING AT?!" yelled Tom in a volume that could be heard by half the house. "YOU—"

"I suggest that you lower your voice and do not draw attention to our conversation... I'll explain if you let me."

"It better be good. Telling the prof Alice and I were having it off—"

"Having it...? He must have come to that conclusion from his own doubtful logic. I didn't say anything about romantic liaisons—"

Attracted by Tom's shouting, Nadia, quickly followed by Alice, burst open the door.

"Romantic liaisons? What's this all about?" demanded Nadia. Alice coloured up.

"Sit down, all of you. I promise I will explain... But we have to keep *quiet*," begged Hen. "The least Prof W hears the better—"

"*Now* you say it," stormed Tom. "But you're the one to spill the beans... You've been a spy all along... All that talk of double agents ..." He turned to the girls and said in a tone of utter disgust. "He has admitted he was the one who snitched on us."

"No. I—"

"You said you weren't on the prof's side," protested Alice. "You told us—"

"If you let me, I'll explain. Sit down." He sat on his chair. Alice and Nadia looked at each other and lowered themselves onto the floor and, eventually, Tom sank onto Hen's bed.

"This better be good," he said, crossly.

"OK. As I said before," began Hen, "I'm with you – all the way. One hundred per cent. Only sometimes you've got to play it cool–"

"Play it cool! Is that what you call it?" protested Nadia.

"Explain," demanded Alice. "As Tom said, it better be good."

"OK," began Hen, half apologetically. "Prof W knew you had been up to something. The night staff had reported the so-called crises with Nadia that turned out to be nothing. They were suspicious. Then they saw wet footmarks on the wooden stairs. They didn't know whose, and they weren't thinking that it was wet from outside–"

"How?–" demanded Alice.

"I heard them through the prof's open door... Listen. When I saw the night staff conferring I knew something was up. I followed them to Prof W's office... You know he *thinks* I'm his spy. *But I'm not.* I only let him think like that so I can glean information. As I said, things are not right here. He's not straight up. But I'll come back to that. I knew sooner or later that they would put two and two together and guess you had been outside. You knew it was risky. I told you it was – you were lucky to get away with it at the time. I was never in favour of it–"

"So you betrayed us," cut in Tom.

"I did *not*. Just listen."

"Let him finish," sighed Alice. "I want to hear this."

"OK. So I overheard what they were saying and I approached the door and knocked. They stopped talking. 'Excuse me,' I said, 'but you asked me to keep you in the picture. I just thought you ought to know. Alice and Tom took off their monitors and then flipped into the fifth, both at the same time. I don't know if they mean to tell you this... Sorry for interrupting.' He just asked, 'Together?' I confirmed it and then I went to breakfast. That's all I said. Nothing else. I didn't want them to work out you had gone for a run. I did it to throw him off the scent. He would have investigated and noticed your monitors had been taken off - then there were all the drips on the stairs and in the hall. I needed to stop that. The romance thing is purely in the prof's warped mind... *I'm on your side.* Honestly."

"Funny way of doing things," remarked Tom. But he had calmed down.

"I know. It's dangerous and it's devious. But I have to keep up the spy thing; the stakes are too high. There's far more to this than appears on the surface. There's something going on that is not right. I don't know what it's all about but it's obvious our prof's desperate. I reckon the reason he came up with the romance idea so fast was that it might give him more clues about where in the brain he might find his 'anomaly'. He's given up behaving logically; he's clutching at straws... Look, I told him from the first day I was here that I can flip whenever I choose, for as long as I choose but what I can't do is *stop* myself from flipping.

"I told him that flipping happens with a surge of excitement – that's the trigger – and that fear, however, dampens it immediately. You get excited and you're off; you get scared and it stops it. But all he's interested in is a specific site in the brain that becomes active. In order to prove his theories, he needs to see a physiological difference between those who flip and those who don't; and I don't think, for one moment, that he has found one. And no results means no breakthrough, no fame and no more money... He's supposed to liaise with a team in the USA but I get the idea that he isn't doing much of that."

"Where does all the money come from? I mean for this clinic?" asked Alice.

"I'm not entirely sure. Some of it comes from the British and European Councils for Medical Research but not all of it by any means. There must be other funders – private ones."

"Why would someone fund the programme privately?" Alice wanted to know.

"Could be a philanthropist. But more likely someone who is investing in order to reap a return later."

"Like what?"

"Treatments. Drugs. Food products. Advertising – all sorts

of things. That's one thing I would like to know... And the other is how long Prof W is prepared to go on getting no results."

"If we leave, he won't get any," put in Tom, sharply.

"Exactly. That's why he is keeping us behind locked doors with our phones in a drawer ... And why everything we say through the computers is monitored. We go, and the whole enterprise collapses."

"So. Why don't you just go?" asked Nadia.

"We can if we have to. But I'm staying here because I need to be with other people like me so I can find out more about flipping... You're the only other people I know who do it. Basically, we need each other; we need to work on this thing. It's interfering with all our futures... yes?" They all nodded. "So we're better in this place together than out for now... What we have to do is get Prof W on the right track. Maybe he can begin listening. But until he does, we can work on this together. We don't need machines to tell us what's happening."

"What can we do to get the prof to listen?"

"I have connections – or rather my parents do. One of them is called Bishop Rowena in New Jersey, USA."

"A bishop! In the USA? That's daft," marvelled Nadia. "That's, like, halfway around the world!"

"The world is a small place these days," explained Hen. "And this bishop holds a brief in The Episcopal Church in America which includes the well-being of teenagers. Dad's going to try to get her in on the case... I write coded messages to my parents."

"Devious again," sighed Alice. But she believed Hen and, somehow, she had forgiven him. He had covered up for them; he could have told the prof everything and he hadn't. She also believed him about Prof W putting two and two together and coming up with the wrong answer; the passion thing hadn't been Hen's invention.

Hen smiled. "OK, I'm devious. But it's being wise, cunning perhaps, but basically under the circumstances... Anyway, this bishop has an office in New York which is only a subway journey from the Long Island Neurological Research Laboratories - the people Prof W is supposed to talk to. So that could work. Meanwhile, we have to go along with the prof and make him trust us."

"Like he does you?" Tom muttered.

"Exactly."

Alice relaxed. "I'm glad you're on our side, Hen... If you are," she added.

"I am. Honestly. We need to share all we know about this. We need each other. I miss my school, but I need to be here with you three. With practice and experimenting, we could do all sorts of things. But it won't be through our professor's current regime because he won't listen to us."

"So why don't we just leave and do our own thing?" asked

Alice.

"Because," explained Hen, "we'd all be sent in different directions - isolated from each other without any chance of learning from other 5Ds."

"If you lot left, I wouldn't stand a chance," mumbled Nadia, half to herself.

"Don't worry, Nadia. We're staying," Alice heard herself say. She truly missed her family but being with these people, she realised, was really important. "I'm not like Roxanne, I'm not going to run away... What was it with Roxanne anyway?"

Nadia looked uncomfortable. "She didn't just leave ... Look, I'll tell you ... later. I will tell you. Not now. It's just good to know you ain't going to do a bunk."

"So, Hen, you are definitely on our side then," confirmed Alice.

"How can I be on the side of a man who is doing nobody any good? But as long as he thinks I'm a devoted subject, then I have much more leverage... Look, I promise I'll dispel his false assumptions about your romantic liaisons. I'll 'report in', saying that you really weren't doing anything like that - I'll say I was there when you flipped. I shall say that you are too scared of him to argue with him and you let him think what he wanted."

Alice sighed. "It really doesn't matter what he thinks. I don't care unless you, Tom..." she looked across at him.

"It makes no odds to me," he shrugged.

Nadia, who was now feeling as if a huge weight had been lifted from her with everyone saying they weren't going away, got the giggles.

Soon they were all laughing. Life suddenly got better...

"Grab hold!" commanded Hen. "Remember what I told yooooo–"

The next thing they knew was that they were on the sloping plane of the fifth. Tom was missing at first, but they soon spotted him and caught him up as they walked alongside an ellipse. They communicated through their hands – there was no way they could make sounds. There were sounds – soft ones – but they all seemed to be a jumble of stuff that calmed down somewhat as they concentrated on just being there, together. Being in the 5D state was not so bad when you were with others, not that it had any beauty or anything. It was a dull flat monochrome place where nothing happened. It just existed. It would be pretty boring if that was all there was. But maybe, just maybe, they could discover something more in it now they were gaining confidence. And the wonderful thing was they were now coming to really believe they were not sick – just different.

25

230 miles north-east of Padget's office in Washington DC, Bishop Rowena Fontaine sat at her desk in 815 Second Avenue, New York City, the headquarters of the Episcopal Church.

"How did it go with Congressman Sparksky?" asked Angela, her administrator in the department of Young Adult Concern with whom she shared an office.

"Er... he was pretty dismissive. Told me to keep my nose out of politics - things that shouldn't concern me. You know the sort of thing."

"That old chestnut. What did you tell him?"

"I told him that the Episcopal Church has the interests of all young people at heart, but he laughed and as good as said that all I was interested in was recruiting new teenagers for my irreligious denomination. I told him the Episcopal Church was concerned for the welfare of all young people whatever their religion or none, whether they are black or white, rich or poor and irrespective of their gender or sexual orientation. I said Jesus calls us to love our neighbour - which means everyone, no matter what. To which he just grunted."

"So what did he have to say about the education bill?"

"I asked him if he had thought to look at it from the point of view of a sixteen-year-old."

"And..."

"And he said you don't ask a cow to design a milking parlour. But I pointed out that young people are not cows. You can't talk to a cow – she wouldn't understand you. But with sixteen-year-old human beings, that's not the case. And, anyway, even with cows, if you don't try to put yourself in their place then you're going to design something that's not fit for purpose and the cows won't take to it. The trouble is he knows what *he* wants and isn't interested in the kids. I told him what young people want is space – space to find out who they are and what opportunities they want to pursue, not a more crowded curriculum with more exams at the end of it."

"I bet he didn't like that."

"No, he didn't. 'If you don't train a child,' he told me, 'they will become wayward. Discipline and hard work are what is required. They must follow a clear and well-marked path. And if their parents, schools and churches are willing to allow children to choose things for themselves, they will go astray.' There seemed little point in trying to tell him sixteen-year-olds are not children that require being shackled and pumped full of knowledge."

"You didn't get anywhere, then?"

"Well, who knows. I said there were lots of sad examples where young people's lives have been wrecked by being over-worked and over-disciplined. I said it can turn some of them into monsters. But he quit at that. I think he began to think of his own kids ... So what's next on the agenda, Angela?"

"You have a couple of hundred emails, but only ten that are not adverts or diatribes... What do you know about the fifth dimension?"

"The fifth dimension? Is this sci-fi?"

"No. Apparently scientists have long believed there are many more dimensions to be found the deeper you go inside the building blocks of atoms, but they are too small for us to notice. However, some people – young people – have been what they call 'flipping into a fifth dimension'. Some doctors suspect that it leads to some losing their lives but it is often put down to accidents – coming off bikes, falling off train platforms and the like. Some, however, survive to tell the tale... The father of one British fifteen-year-old, supposedly a survivor, says he knows you."

"Me? Who is he?"

"A Sebastian Hengrove-Blunt. He says he's—"

"A civil engineer in the UAE."

"Abu Dhabi. You remember him?"

"Who can forget a name like that?" Bishop Rowena smiled. "Yeah. He gets about a bit. He's a member of an international consortium with an office here in the Big Apple. I met him at a convention. He's one of those who builds milking parlours from the cows' point of view. You should see the pictures of the fantastic school he's designed out there in the desert. What's he want?"

"Apparently," said Angela, reading from the email, "his son Christopher is one of the people he calls the 5D survivors. He says Christopher has had to leave his English public school – which in Britain, of course, means fee-paying – because he keeps flipping into the fifth dimension. He's currently in a clinic in London but he's worried that things there are not as they should be. He goes on to claim that the boy and his fellow inmates are getting nowhere fast. The point is that this clinic, the Winterford Clinic in London, is supposed to be working closely with the Long Island Neurological Research Laboratories in Queens. But his son doesn't think that is happening."

"This sounds interesting," said the bishop, intrigued. It made a change from exam woes. "You say this condition affects teenagers rather than adults?"

"Apparently," answered Angela. "I've done a bit of research. There isn't much to find, though. But according to your UAE friend, there are probably a lot more cases than those that have been so far recognised."

"Wouldn't this have attracted media attention?" asked

Rowena.

"Doesn't look like it," shrugged Angela. "Mr Hengrove-Blunt says this clinic deals with all sorts of people with brain conditions like epilepsy and his son isn't getting a good deal. I'll forward you his email..."

Bishop Rowena replied to Sebastian Hengrove-Blunt saying that she would look into the situation and, if she got an opportunity, perhaps visit the Long Island Neurological Research Laboratories and keep him posted. The idea of young adults flipping into a new dimension was quite amazing if it were true. She was sceptical but true or otherwise, it represented just another thing for young people to deal with. Teenage pressure.

Whatever a congressman might call her for doing it, the bishop for Young Adult Concern was not going to abandon her campaigning; she half expected him to cast her a slur via Twitter or something. If he did, it would only add to the publicity. She looked up to the wall where a big notice hung for all visitors to see. It was a picture of the night sky – star-spangled space – with the words scrawled across it like graffiti and at the bottom in small letters, a quotation from the Bible that ran:

"Then shall the young women dance and be happy,
and the young men and the old shall rejoice together."
Jeremiah 31:13

JESUS comes to give you SPACE!

So give our kids room to GROW
to be all they can be.

And then, for God's sake,
LISTEN to them!,

In a box in the corner was the explanation:

**Like a true friend, God doesn't CROWD you
as He sets you free to change the world with
LOVE.
He doesn't load you with
IMPOSSIBLE EXPECTATIONS.
He comes to make ROOM for you to
explore, discover and become
who YOU are –
who you REALLY can be!**

26

Weighed down in deep thought, Prof W was walking slowly towards his laboratory when Hen called out to him. "Professor. Professor. Sorry to interrupt but I thought you should know ... Alice and Tom say you think they... that they were... engaged in... indulging in... caught *in flagrante*... They weren't. I was there."

The professor stopped dead, turned and looked Hen straight in the face. He was angry.

"You led me to believe—"

"I only said they had taken off their monitors and flipped together... I thought it important that you knew because it could skew your results."

"It could indeed. So if they weren't... what *were* they up to then?"

"They were laughing. Tom dared Alice to get him a glass of water out of the kitchen without being seen while Nadia distracted the night staff. She did but spilt it all down his trousers. They laughed so much that they flipped."

"Why didn't they tell me this?"

"They're... they're scared of you. They said they thought

they would get into more trouble tricking the night staff and getting water on the stairs than being engaged in a romantic episode... Apparently, you said you weren't concerned about the rights and wrongs of that."

"Scared?... of me?"

"You are rather more strict than they're used to. They've never lived away from home like me."

"All right. Thank you, Christopher. I'm grateful to you." But the professor seemed crestfallen.

"You know. If you want us to flip more... One way would be to take us out," suggested Hen, tentatively.

"Out? Outside?"

"We have all been active people."

"Well, I suppose we could go to the swimming baths... Do they swim?" asked the professor.

"Tom definitely does. I guess Alice and Nadia wouldn't mind whatever it is... They might even flip at the mention of a trip out."

"Thank you, Christopher. I'll look into that."

27

At dinner time Tom, Alice, and Nadia were sitting together finishing their pudding when Prof W came over, drew up a chair to the open end of the table, turned it around and sat with its back up against his chest. He was making an effort to "be nice". Yuk. Hen had already filled the others in on the conversation he had had with Prof W that morning - both his debunking of the prof's romance conclusion and his suggestion of an outing.

Alice thought this informal Prof W was quite amusing and she did her best to stifle a giggle by pretending to choke on her apple pie.

"Hi guys!" he began. Alice spluttered. "Now. I have a proposition to make. You have all been very good and kept indoors for a few weeks." Alice spluttered again. Now she was really choking on her pie.

"Sorry!" she got out eventually.

"I know it's been hard," continued the professor - he seemed more embarrassed than he was embarrassing, "but we had to have the best results we could. But now, I think we can have an outing. I have already mentioned the idea to Hen and he thinks you might like it."

Alice screwed up her toes and tried to look surprised. It worked. Prof W didn't suspect Hen had already said anything.

"What do you say about a trip to the leisure centre at Swiss Cottage? They have a teaching pool there where you can have fun in the water without having to go out of your depth – safer if you flip. I have looked into it. They are open in the evening. We could get the night staff to take you. In fact, I could come myself – just to make sure you're safe. We don't want to draw too much attention if you flip in public view."

"Yeah," said Tom. "I fell in the sea when I flipped for the first time. I didn't drown because I floated on my back."

Prof W smiled. "We'll all look after each other. How does that sound?"

"Brilliant," replied Alice. "But I don't have a swimming costume with me."

"Me, neither," said Nadia.

"Well then, we shall have to take you to the shops... On the house," smiled the professor.

"Thanks!" exclaimed Alice with real sincerity. Two trips now. *The shops!*

You could see the prof was impressed and thinking to himself how clever he was.

"Right then. Today is Monday. Let's make it tomorrow for

the shops and Wednesday for the swim." He was pleased with himself - and all the while watching to see if anyone was going to flip.

After he had gone, Hen came over and said, "You happy? You see my subterfuge is paying off. Cunning works... And I doubt if he'll ever mention romance to you or anyone again. I bet he feels totally stupid on that score."

"It was clever of you even to account for the rainwater and Nadia's distraction," conceded Alice. "I'm sorry if we misjudged you."

"That's OK. It's par for the course for a spy... So now, the thing is, you've got to flip on these outings."

"You mean, deliberately? I can't just bring it on," protested Alice.

"Have you tried?" Hen asked.

"No. I always just wanted to stop it."

"Exactly," said Hen with authority. "We want to master this... control it. But it's something that is part of us; we need to embrace it... Let's all practice this evening. If we succeed, it'll show up on the monitors and the prof will be even more pleased with himself."

Alice agreed but something about Hen's tone was a bit too bossy. Tom must have thought the same because he said.

"OK. Let's vote on it. All four of us have to decide. We all have to be happy. *All for one and one for all.*"

"Agreed," said Hen.

"Cool," retorted Alice. "I like the musketeers bit."

"Musketeers?" Nadia was confused.

"It's a story," explained Alice. "Three musketeers in France meet a fourth called D'Artagnan and they all promised to stick together. They swore: *All for one and one for all.*"

Nadia grinned. "I don't know what you're on about but count me in for that."

"Let's vote," said Tom. "Hen is to teach us how to bring on a flip after tea. Hands open is yes, a fist is no. On the count of three. One, two, three."

They each thrust a hand forward into the centre of the table. All had their hands palm up and open.

Nadia liked it. "Great. *All for one and one for all!* I've had enough of people deciding for me. No one ain't going to do that no more."

"It's important to make the prof *think* he's getting *his* way, though," said Hen.

"Whilst all the time it's us using this place to do our own thing," laughed Alice. "I like it!" Then she remembered the promised shopping trip. "And a shopping outing's fab. I'm not going to settle on the first cozzy I see," she stated, defiantly. "I'll make them take me into at least three shops. With trying on and everything, it'll take more than half the day."

"Then they'll have to take us to a burger joint for dinner," mused Nadia. "Whoops, I'm going!"

Inside the fifth dimension, Nadia looked around and found Alice. She reached out and caught hold of her. They held each other tightly. Then, gently, very gently, they slid back into the 4D world and were even sitting on the same chairs.

"Hey, that was cool," breathed Alice.

Tom and Hen were missing. They, too, must have flipped. A minute later they reappeared on the floor at the end of the refectory.

"Wow!" said Tom. "We travelled forward in time. Hen showed me how. It's all to do with the black balls."

"I know, we've been sitting here waiting for you," said Alice.

"If only I could *not* go when I don't want to, this could almost be fun," sighed Hen. "The perfect party trick."

But Nadia was thoughtful. Quiet. Something appeared to be wrong.

"What's up, Nadia?" asked Alice.

"It's just I wish Roxanne could have been part of this," she sighed.

"There's something more than you missing her, isn't there?" asked Alice, carefully. "What was it with Roxanne, Nadia?

Why did she leave? It wasn't just that she couldn't hack it and ran away, was it? You're worried about her, aren't you?"

"Yeah. You're right. I haven't told you everything about Rox. Rox's, kind of, mixed up... I don't mean she's crazy, not like that, but I understood her..."

"You're not making much sense," said Alice.

"Listen. That's the trouble, people don't listen enough," protested Nadia. "The prof weren't understanding Rox because he didn't really want to know; he never really listened. Most people don't. It's like you said, Hen, the prof has got his theories and if anything don't fit, then he's not interested."

"Are you saying Roxanne was not a 5D?"

"Sure she was. Rox flipped all the time – much more than me. But that's not the point. She cut herself. The staff didn't want to know. She didn't just leave, the prof threw her out."

"Threw her out because she had an accident?" Tom retorted. "That was unfair."

"No. You see you don't understand either ... you don't know about these things."

"I think I know what you mean," said Hen. "It wasn't an accident. She cut herself deliberately. Her arms?" Nadia nodded.

Alice gasped.

"It's not that uncommon," said Hen. "It happens in our school - mostly among the girls."

"You saying she tried to kill herself?!" exclaimed Alice, shocked.

"No. That's the point. She didn't do it so she would die - not so that she would bleed *that* much. She did it when... when she needed a boost. The thing is, pain can make you feel better."

"I don't get it," sighed Alice. "Pain's bad. How can it make you feel better?"

"Most people don't get it. I do," went on Nadia. "I have never cut myself but I've been in that place - inside myself - where something has to happen to help you kind of break out. The world gets so tight, you can't breathe. Your whole body and your brain hurt - like you're trapped in, inside... It was like that for Rox, only much worse than for me."

The three said nothing. Something about the way Nadia was saying this made them want to listen. It needed to be listened to.

"Rox didn't want to die. Sorry..." Picking up the mood, Nadia apologised. "I didn't mean to upset you... Rox... I just wanted to try to explain. The point is: I reckon she didn't *choose* to leave. The prof kicked her out, just as she found someone - me - to talk to. Someone who could understand a bit - help her find a spark somewhere."

"If Prof W's a brain person, he should know about these things, shouldn't he?" remonstrated Alice.

"The wrong kind of brain person, Alice," answered Hen. "He's a neurologist, not a psychiatrist. He's not interested in a pathology that has been studied for over a hundred years. He's not going to get an award for working in the field of self-harming - even if there is a neurological explanation."

The others didn't really follow all that, but Nadia continued. "The second time she cut herself it was by smashing a window. There was a fight and she barricaded herself in the dining room. By the time I got in, the prof must have taken her through into the laboratories. He sent me back to bed. And then, the next morning, she was gone."

"Chucked out when she most needed looking after," said Tom, quietly.

"Yeah. Now you're getting it," said Nadia. "I don't know nothing about all the fancy stuff the doctors know - or think they know - but Roxanne needed someone... needs someone."

"Do you know where she is?" asked Hen.

"Nah. We were never allowed Snapchat or stuff, were we? Anyway, I doubt she's got a phone... I asked the prof where she were after she had gone and he said he had no idea. He weren't happy about it, I could see that. And I believed him."

There was a pause and then Alice held both Nadia's hands in hers and looked her in the eyes. "Nadia, I promise, we're not going anywhere... But I get it now. It's not all about you, is it?"

Nadia nodded.

"And if we get a chance," promised Hen. "When we've got through here, we'll look for her."

"You mean that?" Nadia looked him in the eyes.

"Definitely. Roxanne needs someone who can understand her. We have to find her... er... if you all agree on that?"

"Sure," agreed Tom.

"Me, too. No problem," confirmed Alice.

Nadia wept. "Thanks... I wish Rox could hear that."

28

Alice was true to her word. They went into three shops and then ended up going back to the first. They got their burgers, too. And Prof W got his reward. It was incredible that this was the first time the man supposed to be in charge of the research actually witnessed any of them flipping. It had never occurred to him that freedom enabled people to be themselves. After the visit to the leisure centre, he appeared to have actually enjoyed himself. He said he was so looking forward to the results of the scans, too. This intensity of flipping was bound to show up.

The next day, the four young people were in the refectory having a well-earned lunch. The previous day's fun and freedom had been worth all the extra testing they had had to undergo that morning. As the four relaxed in the refectory, their professor was eating a sandwich in his office, skimming through some of the new computer readouts. He was in a good mood. Not only had he got the youngsters to flip, but he had also made them happy – and the happy kids made him feel happy.

"No. I'm not staying for a yoghurt today," stated Nadia. "I ain't saying they're not good for you – but they're so boring... I'm going to my room. I'm going to start reading *The Lie Tree* you gave me, Alice... You know, I never read much at home. Now it's most of what I do between the poking and prodding."

Within a day of the outings, they were getting bored again. Alice couldn't stop thinking about her family. She had kept up all the time with formal emails that had to be exchanged the same time every day. She rang on Sundays. That was unnatural – she had never sat at home and talked at length with her parents. *When you live with someone you just do and say stuff as it happens*, she reflected. She got to dislike the routine of Sunday's call at three o'clock sitting on an upright chair in the computer room. She sensed her parents' strain, too. They missed her and they were worried about her and she had to spend a lot of the time trying to reassure them. It was back to the pretending thing again. It was hard work but what else could she do? She was committed to being at the clinic and did not want them to take her home – which they would have done at the first hint of her being unhappy.

Hen Skyped his parents – that was normal for him – but found himself left out of the daily interchanges with his school chums. Their texts gradually petered out because he couldn't react straight away and by the time he got to the computer room everything had moved on. Alice managed better with her friends but it was still a problem. She found she didn't know what they were on about some of the time.

Tom phoned his mother on a Friday. His calls were less than ten minutes long and he didn't mind anyone listening in.

Nadia never seemed to bother about her dad at all. She didn't have a phone and declined the use of Alice's. Alice thought it odd but didn't say anything; she knew Nadia's life was complicated.

"I'll give the yoghurt a miss too," said Hen, getting to his feet.

"Off to do some more spying?" teased Alice. The last few days had seen a decided improvement in their relationship.

"Of course... when I've done my maths session." His college was sending him twice the amount Alice was getting. At first, they thought the clinic would provide some sort of tutor but nothing had materialised. Apparently, Prof W had said he would do it himself but he never did.

Tom had already started his yoghurt and Alice was licking her lid.

"You never lick the lid," smiled Alice. "Too well brought up?"

"Hardly."

"Look, now we're alone..." began Alice, "I've been meaning to say... All that stuff about... you know, the romance thing. I mean, it's not about you. What made me angry was that it was only because all the prof seemed to care about was his experiments. He didn't care about it being morally wrong or anything. So if I seemed off, it's not because... well, I don't like you or anything. I don't want you to feel, like, I was upset by the thought..." Alice stammered to a halt. How should she put this without actually coming on to him? She breathed deeply and sighed. Tom was watching her, saying nothing. "The truth," she resumed, "is that, with all that's been happening to me, I just haven't been thinking about that sort of thing... with anyone."

Tom smiled. "I know. Same here... The thing is, my mum would be mad if I got a girlfriend that lived, like, hundreds of miles away in the north of England. I'm supposed to get a job locally and find a local girl and live around the corner in West Bay. Mum talks about babysitting her grandchildren, would you believe?... and I'm only fifteen!"

"She wants you to have kids?"

"Yeah. Well, eventually – but not too long in the future. Her parents are dead. My dad and his parents, too. I'm all she's got. And we're not that close."

"Do you want to? I mean get a local job and find someone and settle down forever in West Bay?"

"No way! What I want is to go to sea," said Tom, with an expression of someone who had made up his mind. "Not like my dad and his parents – fishing's had its day. What I really want–"

"Is to own a racing yacht and circle the globe!" exclaimed Alice.

"That will never happen. You've got to be seriously rich to own one of those things, but I would like to crew one."

"But you can't if... if you're likely to flip at any time..."

"It stinks, doesn't it? I guess I shall just have to take the local option, working in a shop or train as a plumber and stick near mum. That'd make her happy."

"No, you can't. You'd go mad!" Alice was feeling his pain. "Look, Tom, you can't choose stuff just to please other people all the time. You'll be like a plant growing in the wrong kind of soil – it'd kill you."

"You know, Alice, I've never met anyone like you. You get people. The girls in my year, the ones that I bother with that is – which aren't many – are all set to become hairdressers if they can't be models, which is hardly likely. They don't *think* about stuff like you do."

"They're happy?"

"In their way, yeah. I suppose."

"But their way is not your way?"

"No... I've never talked to anyone much about being me. In fact, I haven't really asked myself what being me actually is.

Funny thing..."

"What's funny?"

"That I can talk like this about myself to someone else at all. I couldn't imagine doing it with any one of my friends in West Bay. And the really funny thing is, it seems normal with you... I trust you. You're different."

"We're both different, Tom. Since we've been here, we can never see the place where we used to live in quite the same way. Even my best friend, Becky, seems, like, trivial at times. But I wish I could be sure of who I am and what I want. At least your friends know that they want to be hairdressers – I haven't a clue... The thing is," continued Alice, quietly, "I'm confused. School was such a big thing. I was doing OK in lessons. But even with the stuff they send me, I'm bound to be getting right behind. Take French, for instance. I used to be quite good at it, but how can you teach yourself something like that from a book? You need someone to practice with."

"You didn't say. I can speak French."

"You can speak French?!"

"I've never lived anywhere but West Bay but my grandparents were French. It was during the Second World War. My pappi was a fisherman from St Vaast – that's on the coast on the other side of the Channel. When the Germans arrived, it was OK at first. He used to supply them with tasty stuff and they let him carry on fishing. But then he got wind that they were going to requisition his boat. After that, his family would have been destitute like a lot of the others. That same night he put his wife and their baby – my uncle – on his boat and they sailed out of the harbour to do a bit of night fishing. But they kept going, all the way to England. After the British decided he was not a spy, he was given his boat back and they moved to West Bay to fish for the British."

"So your mother's French?" asked Alice, never before imagining Tom was anything but English.

"No. Mum's British – she was born in Dorset after the war," explained Tom. "My grandparents took British citizenship. But around their house, they always talked French – even with my dad. I learned it as a nipper... And I still talk French with my mum sometimes – it makes her feel better. She misses her mum and dad.

"*Maintenant, il faut parler français, eh? Si tu souhaites?*" Alice heard the most lovely French. It wasn't at all like an Englishman speaking it. Tom was sort of transformed into a Frenchman!

"Oh dear," said Alice, rather crestfallen. "I'm afraid you'll think I'm naff. Compared to the rest of my class I was good but you're... like a native of France–"

"Hey!" Nadia shouted through the door. "Hey you two, come and clock this. Get a load of this!"

"*Allons-y, Alice... Voyons voir ce qui se passe!* Let's go and see what Nadia's on about," laughed Tom. "And then you can show me your French textbook and I'll know where you've got to. We can work through it together and you might even get better than your class-mates."

29

Nadia called Alice, Hen and Tom up the stairs to her bedroom window. A large black BMW had drawn up outside the gates and a driver with a chauffeur's cap was standing by the buzzer talking to Mr Potts, the security man. They watched as the chauffeur returned to the car and drove it onto the gravel drive inside the gates that were now closing behind him. The only vehicles they had ever seen do that before were white vans that had backed in with a delivery, or tradesmen come to mend something.

A suave-looking gent, middle-aged, portly and suited, pulled himself out of the back seat as the chauffeur held the door for him. Who could this be?

"Fancies himself, don't he?" said Nadia in the broadest Bristol accent she could muster. Hen joined them; he had torn himself away from his maths to explore the excitement.

Hen peered over Nadia's shoulder. "Could be one of our mystery financiers," he speculated.

"Well, he's got some money that's for sure," remarked Tom. "Doesn't spend it racing a yacht, though – too fat. If he owns anything that floats it would be a cruiser with a crew."

"There. An opportunity for you," joked Alice.

"Statistically, it is unlikely that he has any connection with the sea," said Hen, dreamily.

"He's well-heeled though, ain't he?" stated Nadia, bluntly.

They heard Mrs Brean usher him in as if he were royalty and they went out onto the landing to watch him in the hallway. Mrs Brean was behaving quite oddly. She showed the visitor into the director's office. Then, glancing up the stairs with the sourest of faces and gesticulating wildly, she tried to shoo the four young people back to their rooms. Alice was amazed that the same person could look so different in just a single second – treacle for the visitor, lemon juice for them. She didn't doubt which was the real Old Brean. None of the four made any sign of moving but Mrs Brean ignored them. She rushed off, presumably in search of the professor.

After several minutes, Prof W appeared looking flustered and wearing an odd expression. He did not notice the residents watching him from the second-floor landing. He stopped outside his office, pulled back his shoulders, tugged at his jacket, straightened his tie and flattened his hair. Finally, he tried all sorts of faces in the hall mirror before deciding on a fixed serene smile. Nadia almost got the giggles; it was so comic.

"I think I'm going to flip," she sighed, softly. But she didn't. All four continued to watch as the director opened his office door as if nothing in the world was bothering him.

"Donald! What a pleasure. What brings—" the door shut and they heard no more.

"I'd give anything to hear what they're talking about," mumbled Nadia.

"That may be possible. Just keep quiet," said Hen.

"You're not—?" began Alice

"Shh!" Hen put a finger to his lips.

Mr Potts was outside talking to the chauffeur as Hen made his way to the security desk in the lobby, pressed a couple of buttons and turned a knob then returned up the stairs.

"I've turned on the CCTV in the prof's office. It's recording – it's one of those with a sound option."

"Won't they notice?" Alice wondered.

"Only if they look up and see the small red lights," explained Hen.

"What about Mr Potts?" Tom wanted to know.

"I'll try and turn it off before he gets back," said Hen, "Anyway, even if he spots it, he'll never guess I turned it on deliberately. Look, he's taking the chauffeur around the back to give him tea or something."

"A posh *latte* more like," suggested Nadia.

"I'll just pass by and turn it off when it looks as if the chap is coming out," said Hen.

"You're definitely destined for MI6," joked Alice in a whisper.

Nadia giggled. It wasn't much, but compared to the usual boredom, someone who made the director look like a TV comedy clown was something.

"That fella's got more faces than an octopus," she laughed, in the safety of Tom's first-floor room.

"An octopus only has one face - eight arms but one face..." observed Tom.

"You know what I mean, he can twist it about... You never know what the prof's thinking."

"You're right," agreed Alice. "He's always acting... I wonder what he's really like, inside?"

"Could be a strangler," ventured Nadia. "A squashy face and eight arms to grab you round the throat!"

"Don't joke! For all we know, he could be anything..." shuddered Alice. "I don't like the look of him. He's creepy. I don't trust him."

"Hen didn't trust him from the start, did you?" said Tom. "You're wise."

"Devious," corrected Nadia.

"As I said before," broke in Hen, "you just have to try and get one step in front of people like our professor... and I think we're just about to do that."

155

After no more than fifteen minutes, Padget emerged from Prof W's office. The teenagers watched from their station on the second-floor landing as Mrs Brean swept towards him to see him out.

"Allow me—"

"Where's that man of mine, woman?" demanded the entrepreneur.

"Er. Your chauffeur? Having tea in the kitchen. I'll get him." She made her way to a green baize door behind the stairs. Prof W followed her. "A word, Mrs Brean," he said, politely and disappeared from the friends' view, leaving Padget alone in the hallway.

Hen chose that moment to pad down the stairs. He made to pass by and, as he did so, put his hand over the security officer's desk pretending to pick up a book. While his hand was there he pressed the button to cease the recording.

"So who are *you*?" Padget asked. Hen turned towards him, looking nervous.

"Er, the name's Hengrove-Blunt... I'm a resident here..." he replied, almost apologetically.

"So you go on trips, eh?"

"Trips? We rarely get out, I'm afraid—"

"Not *that* kind of trip, son," barked Padget.

Hen, pretended to misunderstand."Oh, I see. Never. I

assure you, I don't take drugs. I never have."

Padget wore an expression somewhere between anger and exasperation. "But you travel into the *fifth dimension?*"

"Ah, yes... Er, something like that... yes."

"Is it fun, boy?" drawled Padget, sarcastically.

"No! We are here to get better."

The entrepreneur laughed. "What you are here for, boy, is to make me a lot of money," he joked.

"I'm sorry? Money? I don't understand." Hen feigned innocence and ignorance. Alice watched him from above with a mixture of admiration for his cunning and acting skills, and fear that Padget would see through it.

The professor reappeared from under the stairs and saw Hen. "Mr Padget, allow me to introduce you to—"

"We've already introduced ourselves, Williams. Young man," Padget drawled, turning his back on the professor and looking Hen in the eye, "if I were you, while you're here I would keep your head!" And he laughed heartily at his own irony.

The chauffeur appeared at the door. "Be seeing you, professor. November. You have a nice place!"

The chauffeur held the car door open for his master and he got in. Mrs Brean and Prof W watched as the car began to reverse.

"The cheek," uttered the housekeeper.

"One day," shook Prof W. "One day..." he stormed into his office and slammed the door.

Mrs Brean scowled at Hen. "I told you to make yourself scarce."

"Right-o. Of course." Hen mounted the stairs two at a time and rejoined the others in Nadia's room from where they watched Padget being driven out of the driveway.

"That man's scary," murmured Nadia.

"I think we have found our villain," said Hen with satisfaction. "I can't wait to watch that tape."

30

On a fine May afternoon, Bishop Rowena got off the subway and emerged onto a spacious avenue with flat-topped buildings just two storeys high. She noticed the sky – lots of it. It was nice to get out of Manhattan. In large capital letters, above one of the ground floor shops, she read the words: "SPACE FOR RENT". Space indeed. She wondered how much space was being given to the local spaced-out young people.

Rowena decided to walk the fifteen minutes to the Long Island Neurological Research Laboratories Inc. along wide tree-lined avenues with low sprawling houses and expansive lawns. Here the air was clean and the sound of the traffic muted. She became aware of the clack of her shoes on the sidewalk – something she hadn't heard in a long time.

Although she worked mainly from her office in Manhattan, Rowena was an assistant bishop in the Episcopal Diocese of North Jersey which earned her an apartment in Newark. It fronted onto a busy street with a couple of stunted trees and a hundred trucks an hour at peak times. Rowena's national brief took her away from personally organising the local diocesan youth events; she didn't need to live where she did but she didn't regret it because it enabled her to be aware of the challenges of urban America first hand. And young people from her diocese had challenges aplenty. This part of Queens she now found herself in, however, seemed to be on a different planet.

Apart from a central glass cuboid, the LINRL buildings were low single-storey blocks surrounded by parkland. The bishop mounted the steps to the glass atrium and found the reception desk under the shade of a potted palm. The woman behind the desk smiled broadly.

"Welcome. Have you an appointment?"

The bishop introduced herself but before the receptionist had time to buzz him, Professor Bradford was crossing the floor to greet his guest.

"Bishop. Welcome to our facility. We are most honoured."

"Thank you, professor. I'm impressed with your, er... place."

"We are indeed most fortunate – a lot of people care about neurological research. But my own department is a bit of a departure. We began by being... well, come to my office and I'll explain properly." He led Rowena back through the main entrance and along a path to a simple wooden building among trees.

"It's a softer setting. It suits our subjects better than glass and steel – makes them feel more comfortable."

Seated on a long pale-brown sofa, the professor outlined the research with which he had been engaged over the previous ten years.

"We began by assuming the 'events', as we are wont to call them, related to some kind of brain condition," he began. "Perhaps a kind of epilepsy or a similar lesion. We also considered an infection – a virus or bacteria or even a parasite."

"You mean some kind of alien creature?"

"You make it sound like science-fiction," smiled the professor. "No. We didn't consider anything from outer space if that's what you mean. But there are numerous biological entities on the Earth that can get inside the human body and invade its structures."

"But you didn't find any?"

"Nothing that would cause the kind of fits or attacks that had been observed.

"About five years ago, however, I witnessed something that convinced me that people were experiencing events that were not just neurological. I was privileged to observe someone undergo one such episode from beginning to end.

"This subject described to me what I now identify as the classic description of what has become known as a '5D flip'. From this evidence, I changed my basic assumptions. All the flippers showed up as completely normal when scanned – the fifth dimension did not appear to be a product of a brain malfunction... You know, bishop, a good research scientist needs to be able to think outside the box."

"Do call me, Rowena, professor. So—"

"If I am to call you, a bishop, Rowena, then you had better call me Red." The professor grinned.

"Red. So, these patients – subjects – were sort of going somewhere else for a split second – body as well as mind?"

"Exactly. And when they were back they showed no signs of the kind of neurological distress we associate with fits. They just carried on where they had left off. We found we were not calling on doctors but counsellors to help them come to terms with the implications of flipping into a strange dimension. They are all helping us in our research."

"And are all of your subjects teenagers?"

"All but two out of nearly two hundred," nodded the professor, grimly.

"Guys and girls?"

"Equal numbers, and from all walks of life: rich, poor, black, white, academic, practical, sporty, geeky types, musical, extrovert, introvert, bookworms, film-buffs, vampire-slayers, and even churchgoers," smiled the professor. "But nearly always young."

"So what do you do with these young people? You can't keep all two hundred of them here."

"No. We are not a hospital. We only keep people overnight if we want to monitor them over a twenty-four hour period."

"So where are these young people?" Rowena couldn't imagine them walking around flipping all over the place. She would bound to have come across it.

"At home, mostly. I'm afraid they don't get out and about like their friends. They need to be with those who understand them. We teach them, and those they live and study with, how to manage the flipping. After a short while, they generally learn to cope." Professor Bradford appeared to be genuinely moved.

"We are a neurological research centre," he continued, "but these young people are not in need of medical care... not in my opinion. Yet we had nowhere else to refer them, so I fought the management to let me devote my time to researching the phenomenon. I persuaded them to construct this small wooden building where our subjects can meet together, share their experiences and get the counselling they need."

"It must be hard for them?"

"It is," the professor agreed. "They often get called freaks. Sometimes their parents are the least understanding. We need to protect them from that – counsel them, affirm them—"

"Tell them that being them is OK."

"Absolutely. You know, Rowena, I think you and I are going to get along just fine. The truth is that we are coming to think of them not as people with a problem but people with potential... But we have a long way to go to understand what that is. There is so much about this phenomenon to discover and we have barely begun."

"Thanks, Red. One last question. I believe you have a colleague working in London. What role does he play in your research?"

Prof Bradford grinned. "I wondered whether you were going to get onto him. It's through one of his subjects that you have got to hear of the condition."

"Yes. It's complicated but we know each other through the Anglican networks. He lives in the United Arab Emirates. His son is in Professor William's clinic... Can I speak in confidence?"

"Of course. Nothing goes beyond this room."

"The thing is, this boy's father is not convinced he's receiving the right treatment. He's even suggesting that he may be in danger."

"Can I share something with the same kind of confidence, Rowena?" The bishop nodded. "Professor Williams and I have not been singing off the same page for five years – ever since

I came to believe there was not a physiological explanation. He has invested a lot into his clinic. He has gambled everything on a successful outcome to his specific research. If it turns out, to put it frankly, that he has been barking up the wrong tree, then he will lose all funding for his clinic, which is technically owned by him but which - I rather suspect - belongs to the banks. And, at his age, he is unlikely to get a job in any other research department. If he succeeds and proves his theory, Rowena, it would be sensational - a Nobel prize even. It's cutting edge science - it's 'sexy'. But there will be no Nobel prize for someone like me whose research is on the boundaries of the paranormal. I confess that my subjects - those who flip - know much more about what this is about than I do...The thing is: Williams may not be conscious of what he's doing but he is using young people for his own ends. He is preying on their vulnerability. Don't get me wrong; I don't think he *means* them any harm. I am sure he is not consciously abusing them. But he has a number virtually incarcerated in his clinic to forward his own ambition... I am talking in confidence. I reckon I can trust you."

"Of course. I think I might find an excuse to travel to Europe and drop in on this Professor Williams if he will have me."

"Do. But don't tell him you have met me - not until you have got into his facility at any rate - otherwise, he mightn't let you in. I'm glad you came, Rowena. May God bless your plans... or perhaps I oughtn't to ask God to bless a bishop."

"Oh yes, you should. Bishops need as many, if not more prayers than anyone; and I certainly need yours for this... When I get back from London, I'll report back."

"Right. Good... So, where are you headed now? Are you staying in Queen's? It's a long way back to Newark."

"I shall read on the train. I'll be home in no more than an hour."

"Because, if you were staying, I'd offer to take you out for dinner."

"Professor Bradford, are you asking me out on a date? I may be married."

"I don't think so. No wedding ring. If a bishop were married she would wear one."

"Very perceptive of you. I am flattered but charming as you are, I have to make my escape. This evening I have a meeting with the director of youth ministries in Newark to brief me on where they are with the latest youth events. I may travel far and wide, but I am still paid by the Diocese of North Jersey."

"Another time maybe..."

The professor walked Bishop Rowena towards the main building. "May I, at least, offer you a lift to the station?"

"Thank you. That would be appreciated."

"My pleasure."

As Red Bradford turned into Jamaica Avenue, he asked,

"If I can be of any help Rowena, don't hesitate to ask. Call me from London if you need anything."

"Sure. Thanks. I'll be in touch," said Rowena. "Thanks for the ride."

31

Bishop Rowena rocked back in her office chair and called across to her administrator. "I think I have decided what I am going to do with my impending holiday."

"About time," said Angela. "Don't tell me, a singles holiday somewhere hot – the Bahamas?"

"That would involve donning a swimming costume. Hardly."

"Hiking in the Rockies, then?"

"I think I'm going to visit my cousins in Europe."

"Stay at the Château Fontaine?"

"Nope. I shall stay in a hotel and pop in. I don't know them well enough to invite myself."

"Very nice."

"And then pop over to London and see if I can get an interview with Professor Williams."

"That's work!" exclaimed Angela.

"Not exactly. London is part of the Province of Canterbury and my brief runs only as far as TEC. I shall be visiting as a friend of a parent."

Angela accepted defeat. "One day, Rowena, you will

have a proper holiday."

"Define a holiday, Angela."

"A vacation – as opposed to a Holy Day – is a period in which you vacate your work in order to do something you enjoy."

"Precisely, Angela. I shall be in neither 815 nor the Diocese of North Jersey. I shall not answer any emails except those in my personal private account or open any letters, and I'll leave my diary here. I shall enjoy my hobby of meeting foreigners. How's that?"

Angela grimaced. "Well, OK," she said. "It's better than nothing. Do you want me to book you a flight? Paris, London? And a hotel?"

"No. It's a holiday. Let's see if I can book something myself," Rowena added. "If you booked it you would know where I was, but now you can truthfully say, 'Europe somewhere. No idea where.'"

"Not even a postcard?"

"Angela!! That's so old hat! This is a *youth* department. Get with it!"

32

It was eleven o'clock in the evening and Hen listened for the night staff to head off to the kitchen. When the coast was clear, he sneaked down the stairs, plugged a headset into the CCTV device behind the security desk and located the taped meeting in Prof W's office. He hid on the floor and listened. No one disturbed him.

Half an hour later he deleted the recording, padded back up the stairs and knocked softly on Tom's door. They were all there waiting for him to report.

"OK," he began. "Basically we've got till November before that unscrupulous investor pulls the plug. It seems the prof is mortgaged to the hilt. It'll only take one thing to go wrong and his fragile empire will collapse; he'll be bankrupt. It's as I suspected. The prof has banked everything on announcing a dramatic breakthrough – not only proof of a fifth dimension but a neurological anomaly in the brains of flippers that causes them to flip. Identifying the cause would usher in the research for a treatment. The leading pharmaceuticals would profit, and that's where this Donald Padget may have his interests. I would Google him except I don't want our prof knowing we know as much as we do. The problem is that the prof doesn't have the scientific evidence he needs: empirical proof. He's desperate to get his hands on the brain of a flipper who has died. If he can be sure that someone has died in the fifth, then he believes a brain dissection would settle it."

"But he's not very likely to find such a brain, is he?" reflected Alice.

"No. Because, as the prof told Mr Padget, there's always some explanation of how the person died that doesn't involve 5D. When someone's dead, he has no way of proving they ever had a 5D flip—"

"Unless one who's using this clinic dies," cut in Nadia. "That's, like, gross, innit?"

"It's worse than that. Unless one of *us four* dies," clarified Hen. "Everyone else that comes here has other things wrong with their brains in some way - things that will complicate any conclusion. He needs people who haven't had fits or brain damage of any kind."

"And none of us is likely to die before November," stated Tom.

"The statistics are wholly against it," agreed Hen. "But the prof's got too much tied up in this to give up until he absolutely has too. In fact, a few more months will not make things any worse for him - bankrupt is bankrupt, dishonour is dishonour - so he might as well hold on to the bitter end - November."

Nadia was horrified. "Do you reckon he'll try and, actually, do one of us in?! I mean, like, imagine..."

"He'll never do that, surely," Alice was shocked that Nadia had even come up with the thought.

"I seriously doubt it," said Hen. "Even the lure of a Nobel Prize would not be enough for murder. No. Our prof isn't the type; he's not the ruthless sort."

"Just stupid," commented Nadia with her arms folded and her face firm.

"He must be clever, though," protested Alice. "You don't get to pass the doctor exams unless you are."

"You're both right," said Hen. "He's clever at science but stupid enough not to see the wood for the trees. We've got until the end of October to work on this ourselves. I reckon we can make some good progress in that time"

"And then we'll get a Nobel prize," asserted Nadia.

"Hardly." Hen laughed. "They don't give Nobel prizes to teenagers – no matter how brilliant a suggestion they come up with."

"Malala Yousafzai got one," Alice pointed out.

"Yes, but that was a Peace Prize, not a science one... No. Whatever we find out will have to be tested and tested again somewhere before any scientist will accept it... But we can do something to help ourselves. If we can find a way, not only to get into the fifth on demand but also to avoid getting into it when we don't want to, then we've virtually cracked it; we can go on to lead normal lives. All we have to do is keep the prof sweet while we're working on it."

"And if we're cute, we can talk him into letting us do things," said Alice. "I mean, I've only just found out that there're loads more things to do in this part of London than a leisure centre and a library. Did you know that London Zoo is within walking distance?"

Nadia did a jig. "No way! Wicked! London Zoo. It's really famous. I love zoos. Do you really think he would let us go there?"

"If he's going to let us do stuff, I can't see why not," said Alice. "And just down the road there is Madame Tussauds – you know the waxworks museum – and the London Planetarium, too."

"Wow!" reacted Tom. "And what about the boat show?"

"I don't know that one," answered Alice, gently. "Is that in London?" Tom shrugged.

"What you haven't mentioned is Lord's cricket ground which is very nearby," contributed Hen, with authority.

"That's something," Tom affirmed. "You mean we could actually get to watch live cricket?"

"Yes. My Dad has friends who are MCC members. They could probably help us get tickets–"

Hen stopped talking; he had got a feeling someone was standing outside the door. He looked up. A light was on in the corridor and a slight shadow was playing through the gap under the door. Hen raised his finger to his mouth and began talking again.

He gesticulated that Tom should answer him and keep talking. "So you like cricket, Tom?"

Tom got the message and went rabbiting on about the wonders of cricket and the great moments of his school cricketing career while Hen got to his feet and tiptoed towards the door. Then he took hold of the knob and swung the door open and in fell none other than Prof W.

"Oh. Sorry, professor!" exclaimed Hen, genuinely surprised. How much had he heard? "You have come to see Tom?"

"Erm," began the professor, trying to adjust to the shock of being discovered. "I heard a noise. I wondered if you were... if you were all right... Er. What are you all doing here? Is it not time you were in bed?"

"We were just talking about the things we used to like to do," explained Hen. "You know it is hard for young people stuck indoors. Tom and I were talking about cricket and Nadia about her love for zoos. Alice thought that we can't be very far from London Zoo here... But you're right, we should be getting some sleep."

"It's not about being strict with your routine," stated the professor, regaining some of his authority, "it's about knowing what and where so we can monitor you. Would you really like to go to the cricket ground?"

"Yes, of course," said Hen. "I suppose I support Middlesex as much as any county... but I think the girls would prefer the zoo."

"Why not. We can organise both... so long as you do not hold all-night vigils without me knowing."

Nadia was genuinely pleased. "Thanks!"

"Come on Nadia," commanded Alice. "Let's do as we are bid... Goodnight." And she ushered Nadia out before she could flip.

Once they were on the floor above, Nadia asked in a worried tone, "How much do you think he heard?"

"I don't know, but I don't think it was very much. He couldn't have been standing there that long or Hen would have been aware of him earlier."

33

Life was getting much better at the Winterford. Prof W didn't seem to know how to be less strict without going the other way and becoming embarrassingly ingratiating; sucking up to them and pretending to be a grown-up teenager. But it didn't stop the prof's eyebrows rising when Hen approached with a list. Now the four knew how terrified he was of losing them, they had become bold – especially Alice, who was determined to act the part of the "spoiled brat" as Nadia had dubbed her.

"You think I'm made of money, young man?" Prof W said to Hen as he scanned the list.

"It's just... It's summer. The others miss being at home in the summer. They'll all be tempted to go home if you don't give them a reason to stay... The library doesn't cost anything. Alice does a lot of reading."

The professor knew he was beaten. He said he would accompany the boys to the cricket and monitor them. An exciting game might have an effect on them. It might be worth doing. The zoo would be more mundane – Mrs Brean could handle that.

Mrs Brean was not happy. She didn't approve of her boss's new-found leniency and was a pain from the start. She decided she didn't particularly like zoos, and quite resented the idea of taking two teenagers on an outing which she didn't believe they deserved. The fact was that she simply made up her mind not to like the girls that day. Alice sensed this and it brought the worst out in her. Somehow, being treated like a petulant naughty child made her feel like behaving like one.

She and Nadia giggled and danced about in the queue and had this odd conversation that was supposed to be overheard by a boy just in front of them. He completely ignored them although he must have heard.

Mrs Brean was embarrassed. She couldn't follow half what they were saying but if the truth were known, neither did Alice and Nadia.

For a fleeting moment, Alice asked herself why she was doing this. But the day was hot, Mrs Brean was annoying and Hen and Tom were not there – Alice wouldn't have acted like a little kid if they had been. For whatever reason, Nadia was up for acting silly too, and they egged each other on.

Inside the zoo, the bush babies and lemurs were cute but it was the spiders that were the climax for Alice. She and Nadia were fascinated with them – so interested that they almost forgot about being giddy for ten minutes. Mrs Brean, however, was totally scared of spiders and scorpions. She just didn't want to look but she was reluctant to allow the girls out of her sight. When Alice sussed this she insisted on going around again - and again, a third time. Mrs Brean eventually relented and sat and waited for them outside; she wasn't to see either of the girls for the next hour. Eventually, she picked up the courage to go back into the spiders' house but, of course, the girls weren't there.

Alice and Nadia, now rid of Mrs Brean, suddenly became much more grown up. They had left the spiders by a back exit and went off on their own. They checked out the monkeys and the parrots and eventually found the tigers. There were some baby ones on one side, and through a little tunnel, a second enclosure, where the big male could rest without being disturbed by his family. Alice and Nadia were taken by his size and majestic dignity as he totally ignored the milling crowds of all ages that surrounded his enclosure. There were people with pushchairs and toddlers, young people like themselves, older people, clearly not too old to appreciate the grace of these animals and even an elderly man on a mobility scooter. This gentleman was doing his best to get to see, which was not easy sitting down.

Nadia watched the man manoeuvre his scooter to get a better look. Then she saw a little girl stray from her mother; she had a pushchair with a baby in it and another toddler as well as the girl. She was intent on eating an ice cream and, as she ate, wandered across the path without looking up. The elderly man on his mobility scooter began to reverse. Nadia saw the danger and acted on instinct; she could see a disaster unfolding – the old man clearly hadn't noticed the child. Without thinking, Nadia rushed across, picked up the little girl and swung her up out of danger. Then the reversing scooter hit the back of Nadia's legs knocking her off balance. She clung onto the girl, who was surprised at being picked up, and upset because she had lost her ice cream. Nadia was on the floor but the little girl was safe and on her feet. She ran, screaming, to her mother. Alice went over to Nadia and helped her up.

"You OK, Nadia?"

"Yeah. The girl OK?"

"I saw what happened; you saved her. She's scared but she's not hurt. What about you?"

Nadia pulled herself up. "I'm OK. Nothing broken," she bent down and rubbed the back of her legs.

Then things turned nasty. Both the mother and the man on the scooter turned on Nadia. The woman was shouting. The old man was angry. They both began to blame Nadia for the incident. Alice thought that was unfair. Loads of other people had seen what had happened but they had all just melted away as quickly as they could.

Hearing all the noise, a couple of security people came over and one of them asked if Nadia was all right, while the other listened to the complaints. Nadia had a graze on her elbow and she was still feeling the back of her ankle which had taken the full force of the scooter. The security woman said she would take Nadia to the first aid place. She asked if the girls had an adult with them anywhere and Alice volunteered to go and look for Mrs Brean. Eventually, Alice spotted her still hovering around the entrance to the spiders. When Mrs Brean saw Alice with a troubled expression on her face – the naughty little girl having been replaced with a sensible young person looking for the lady responsible for them – she knew something was wrong.

"Mrs Brean. Nadia's in trouble. The zoo policeman wants to talk to you."

"What? What has she done?" demanded Mrs Brean.

"Nothing. She's done nothing wrong but a mother and an old man are both cross with her for saving a little girl."

"Explain. Where is she?"

As Alice led her through the crowds to the first aid station, she told the story.

"Is Nadia all right?" demanded Mrs Brean now becoming genuinely concerned.

"She's scraped her elbow and her leg hurts but she says she hasn't broken anything."

"Well, I suppose that's something. Nobody else hurt?"

"No. But the little girl would have been run right over if Nadia hadn't acted so quickly."

Mrs Brean found Nadia sitting in a small office with the security guard.

"Ah. You are this young lady's guardian I take it," she said standing and extending a hand.

"Yes, I'm afraid so," said Mrs Brean. "I must apologise. She gave me the slip. Should never have come. They are problem teenagers, I'm afraid."

Alice was livid. She would have protested but the woman clearly found Mrs Brean amusing and Alice was sure she had given her a slight wink over Mrs Brean's shoulder.

"I have taken note of Nadia's version of events. I will leave her here with you if I may for a few minutes while I talk to the complainants." She left them in the office.

"I only picked her up so she wouldn't have been run down," protested Nadia. "He couldn't have seen her – she was too small and right behind him."

"So she wasn't hurt?"

"No. Not at all... she lost her ice cream, though, and it must have been a bit sudden... the mother told me 'to get my filthy hands' off her daughter... as if I was trying to do som'ut to her."

"It was racist," stated Alice, bluntly. "I heard her say... er, use a bad racist word to someone else."

"Don't be over-dramatic!" commanded Mrs Brean. That made Alice angry but she said nothing.

Mrs Brean said they would leave as soon as they let Nadia go and then sat for what seemed an age in stony silence.

Eventually, the security woman returned. She asked them what part of the zoo they were planning to see next.

"We're going straight home!" stated Mrs Brean.

"Oh. That's a pity. You see the complainants have withdrawn their complaints. When I told them I would check the CCTV cameras they decided to 'let you off'... It's lunchtime. Have you eaten?" asked the security woman.

"No," declared Mrs Brean. "But to miss a meal will be an appropriate punishment!"

"If I may be so bold," said the woman, "I think you are being hard on this young lady. She almost certainly saved a child from serious injury. I rather think Miss Simpson should be commended," said the guard.

"She gave me the slip."

"Ah. That's not quite right. But I was going to suggest you came with me and had some lunch with my colleagues and then help feed some animals."

Both Alice and Nadia were delighted. Mrs Brean had been outvoted.

The rest of the day went smoothly. Alice and Nadia behaved like young adults. Mrs Brean couldn't work out quite what had come over them earlier. Alice felt embarrassed. She reflected on how different she could be in different situations with different people; she resolved not to be so silly in future.

☆☆☆

Meanwhile, the cricket wasn't proving to be that exciting even though it was an international one-day match. England won the toss, batted first and failed to make two hundred runs. Their opponents had it all done and dusted with one wicket down after thirty-five overs. Tom and Hen were back in the clinic hours before they expected to be.

The zoo had been a much better outing. The girls couldn't make up their minds who enjoyed the outing more in the end – them or Mrs Brean because she had become quite excited when taken behind the scenes of the nocturnal house.

"I wish she would just stop trying to pretend to be serious all the time – you could see she was all of a flutter when she saw the bush babies," commented Nadia.

"But she doesn't like spiders one bit," laughed Alice.

"You were really cruel when you kept wanting to go round again and again just because you were hoping to see her faint."

"I just wanted her to be herself instead of putting on an act as if she's from Vulcan or somewhere," joked Alice.

"Vulcan? Where's that?" Nadia was confused.

"Oh. It's Star Trek. Pointy-eared people from a planet called Vulcan who are not supposed to show emotions... It's a story; it doesn't really exist."

"Oh. I see," answered Nadia, still none the wiser. "But you can be real cruel at times, Alice. She *has* to put on an act. It's what the prof expects."

They told the story of the little girl and the reversing scooter and Nadia showed off her elbow and a large bruise which had come out on one of her ankles.

"Quite a day, then," said Tom. He would have liked to have been there with them. He had missed the girls, especially Alice.

34

Prof W opened his inbox and found an email from Bishop Rowena. She explained she was working with young people in the USA and had come across talk of fifth dimension survivors. She was intrigued and had been referred to him, so, since she was passing through London, could she come and meet him and perhaps the young residents of the Winterford?

Initially, the prof was alarmed. Was this bishop a spy from the Long Island laboratory? He Googled her and found out as much as he could. She seemed genuine - she was turning up at various youth events and church stuff. The message had come from her administrator whom he also checked out. The prof relaxed. If he could handle the American Donald Padget - just about - he could easily manage a female bishop youth enthusiast. She did not seem to know much - just cared about kids.

He replied with a gushing email saying how grateful he was that someone among the church hierarchy should take an interest in his poor clients for whom he was working to find a cure. He was sure the young people would be pleased to meet her. He warned her that they weren't exactly religious; they had shown no desire to attend worship anywhere.

Bishop Rowena replied herself, suggesting a date and time in three weeks.

Prof W asked Hen what he thought about being visited by an American bishop. Hen gave no indication that he knew where all this had originated. He shrugged his shoulders and said, "Why not? It'd make a change to see someone different."

☆☆☆

The next two weeks were comparatively quiet. In fact, if it hadn't been for their own experiments in the fifth, they would have been positively boring; Prof W had shown no inclination to suggest any more outings. The four were secretly trying to induce and control flips. They devised a way of communicating through sign language whilst in the flat grey world, controlling re-entry and going forward and backwards in time against the black ellipses. They discovered that travelling forward was limited – after a while, they couldn't go any further. The most they achieved was half an hour. Whilst they were there they could come back all the way to the start – well, almost. It could never be earlier than the time they entered, plus the time they spent there – the past was always blocked.

After a few episodes, Nadia grew really bored. "It's always so dull," she commented. "The most useful thing you can do is move on in time a bit, which could get you out of a scrape, but for the rest, it's just grey all the way, innit?"

35

Alice was determined that Nadia's birthday wasn't going to be either grey or flat and published the event as widely as she could. The day in question - the eleventh of June - was going to be a great day. It was the first birthday any of them had celebrated whilst at the clinic. Tom and Alice had both had their birthdays on the first of October and Hen's was mid-November.

Alice cornered Mrs Brean by the green baize door. The woman had been doing her best to avoid Alice and Nadia since the zoo outing - she appeared embarrassed.

"Mrs Brean..." called Alice with her charming face on. "Mrs Brean, it's Nadia's birthday next week - the eleventh. Can we... May we... Would it be possible to have a birthday cake for her? Candles and everything. And perhaps balloons and stuff, too. You see, she's never had a proper birthday with her dad not being... like, up to it."

"A cake? I'll have to ask the professor." Mrs Brean brushed past and continued going - she didn't want to talk to Alice; she looked flustered.

"I'm sure he'll say yes," smiled Alice after her.

He did. He seemed to be getting the message that excitement helped on the flips and this particular proposal did not even involve going out anywhere.

When the day came, Nadia had no idea that anything had been planned for her. In fact, her birthday had meant so little to her in previous years that she quite forgot it. She was still getting dressed when Alice rapped on her door and let out a whoop and a joyous, "Happy Birthday!"

"Yeah..." was all that Nadia managed to say as she let Alice in. Holding onto a half-braided hank of hair she said, "You keen on birthdays? Don't know why."

"Oh, Nadia. Stop being so grumpy. Birthdays are supposed to be fun days and today you're going to have a fun day – we all are."

"Thanks, Alice. I've never had a fun day birthday... Last year Dad never mentioned it – no one did." Nadia checked her braids in the mirror. "Never does what you want it to."

"What? Your dad?"

"Nah. My hair."

Alice stepped up and smiled into the mirror. "Want me to help?"

"You never use braids. You know what to do?"

"Sure. I reckon. I braided all my dolls' hair when I was

ten."

"I ain't no doll!"

"If it's no good, you can always pull it out."

"Guess... OK. After breakfast; to do it properly takes time."
Nadia picked up a plain grey T-shirt from the chair and went to
put it on. Alice protested.

"Nadia Simpson. It's your fifteenth birthday. You only ever
get one of those. It's your great day so wear something bright.
You never wear anything colourful. With your skin, you
should—"

"You saying black ain't beautiful?!"

"No I'm not," protested Alice, playfully. "Black is beautiful.
Just saying grey doesn't go with fudge chocolate! You could
be quite, like, stunning if you put some colour on. Fun day,
Nadia!"

"You're bossy, ain't you?"

"Only when I'm right."

Nadia began to giggle. Then they were both giggling as
Alice opened Nadia's wardrobe and rummaged through her
tops, finally extracting a mint green one with small sleeves and
a boat neckline. It was made from a delicate lace with a flower
and leaf pattern over a lining of the same colour. Mid-length
and drawn in at the waist with a wide ribbon fastened in a
bow at the back; it looked really special. Alice gazed at it with

her mouth open.

"Wow! I just love this. Nadia this is the one."

Nadia stopped giggling and went all serious. "It ain't mine."

"It's in your wardrobe. Whose is it then?"

Nadia shuffled her feet and looked at the floor.

"Nadia?"

"It's... it belonged to Rox."

"I thought they cleared all her stuff, like, from my room. You said—"

"She gave it me. Two days before she went... I told her it was hers. It was special. She said yeah it was, that's why she wanted me to have it. She said this so-called aunt – not really an aunt – bought it. She couldn't stand the woman and was never going to wear it. She said it weren't her colour... She made me put it on and said it was great on me and told me to keep it... But it's too fancy, and besides when she just disappeared... I can't wear it."

Alice shifted her weight onto her other foot and then said in a tone that surprised even her. "You have to wear it, Nadia. Roxanne would want you to. If she were here she would say so. It's like a birthday present."

Nadia shook her head and picked up the grey top.

"Breakfast," she said and led Alice from her room.

In the dining room, Tom and Hen were ready with home-made cards and chocolates.

"Chocolates!" exclaimed Nadia. "When did you get out to get them?"

"We didn't," explained Hen. "We recruited one of the staff – told her exactly what we wanted."

Tom smiled at Nadia's reaction. "We spent some of our communications time online looking through sweets."

"And then dispatched a runner," added Hen. "Hope you like them."

Nadia stared, stunned into silence. She had never had such a posh birthday present. The gold box bore the words "Swiss Luxury Selection" on the lid.

"W...What..." began Nadia. "How can this be for me? Them's, like, real mint, innit? no one gives me posh stuff. Where'd you get the dosh from?"

"I get an allowance," smiled Hen. "And I don't get to spend it, do I? It's just accruing."

"And I got something from me mum to spend, too," added Tom.

"But me? Why me?" protested Nadia.

"Duh! Maybe because it's your birthday!" mocked Alice. "Look, Nadia. We're your friends, right? When you've got friends, you get presents. And I guess you're going to share these."

"I... I... Thanks, guys."

"Happy birthday, Nadia," said Alice loudly. Then the staff came in with cards and presents, too. Even the prof produced a large card and an even bigger box of sweet things which he gave her saying, "Mind you record them on your intake chart."

No one missed either Mrs Brean, who remained hidden behind her green baize door, or the nurse with the pretty daisy pendant.

After breakfast, Nadia allowed Alice to braid her hair and, quietly mouthing a thank you to Roxanne for her present, changed into the green top.

36

The afternoon was hot. The sun was beating down and Tom and Hen were sparring on the croquet lawn. The girls were watching them from the bench under the tree. Mrs Brean came out with a pretty blue envelope for Nadia.

"You have some birthday post, it seems," she announced, handing it to her before retreating quickly back indoors.

Nadia examined it. It bore a Bristol postmark. It couldn't be from her father because he had never given her a birthday card that she could remember. She opened it carefully and pulled out a card depicting a Teddy bear and the words: "For a special daughter." It was from her father.

"Me dad!" she uttered, obviously amazed.

"Nice," said Alice, leaning over. "Great words. He loves you. He misses you."

"T'ain't right. He's never—" began Nadia but she suddenly stopped and slumped on the bench. Alice was alarmed but before any of them could do anything, Nadia sat back up straight again.

"Wow! That was som'ut," she breathed. "How long have I been gone?"

"No more than a couple of seconds," said Alice with a look of concern.

Hen and Tom had detected something happening and came and joined them.

"That was an ace flip," said Nadia. "I was in control. I discovered things."

"Go on," said Hen. "I was inside, like, with the balls but I started to climb up the slope leaving the balls below me. It wasn't hard to get a grip because... because I was thinking happy thoughts. Does that make sense?"

"Probably," said Hen, "Go on."

"I went right up the slope and there was a kind of top to it and above that, it was blue - like the sky. I was way way above the balls and when I looked down I began to slide but I could control the sliding - slow it down by stepping forward. Eventually, when I got level with the balls again, I didn't know where I was - I mean which was my ball - you know what I mean - the one that was passing when I went in? I thought that if I came out in the wrong place I might end up outside or in the future or anything. But it was my birthday and Dad's card was here, so I remembered what you said, Hen, about not being able to go back beyond the point you came in - you can't go backwards into the past, you said. So I thought that if I went back as far as I could I would end up back here on this bench just after I left it. So I did. I must have been in the fifth for what seemed like ten whole minutes at least before I got back to the place where the balls started. I spotted the whirlpool and glided through it."

"And bingo! Right back beside me on this bench," whistled Alice.

"Yeah." Nadia picked up the card that was still in her lap. "I never thought Dad cared... not like this. It's years since I had a Teddy bear, though."

"Your dad chose it because of the words, I expect," said Alice.

Hen was kneeling beside the bench, looking thoughtful. "You said the slope had a top," he said. "Did you reach it – reach the top?"

"Nah, not quite. Almost. I weren't thinking about reaching the top. I suppose I got scared a bit and when I looked down, the bottom seemed a long way away and I thought I should get back," she looked at Hen; had she done the wrong thing?

"That's brilliant," he said, catching her look. "That is a discovery that might be game-changing. And your control is something to be commended. I applaud you."

Nadia looked pleased.

"The thing is," continued Hen, "this confirms our findings: a fourth dimension of time within the so-called fifth."

"And, as we can meet each other, we might be able to

meet other people," suggested Alice. "But what we really want to work on is a way to enter only when we choose – every time... And then we can go home... or whatever," she added squeezing Nadia's hand.

"How long will that take us?" asked Tom.

Hen was confident. "Don't know yet but there must be a way. There has to be."

They remained silent for a minute before Hen spoke. "Come on, Tom. Let's finish our game." They retrieved their mallets and then began debating whose turn it was with which ball.

After a while, Alice murmured half to herself. "I'm glad you're having a special birthday, Nadia, but I really want to be at home for mine when it comes. I hope we can find out enough by next October and I can go home – at least for the day. It seems ages since I was, like, normal."

"Same with me. It seems an age that I saw the rainbow in the gorge," recalled Nadia.

"Nadia," began Alice, tentatively. "Do you want to tell me about that day?"

"I did."

"Yeah. But you left a bit out saying I wasn't, like, ready to know."

"So now you reckon you are?"

"No. I'm not prying. It's just... it's the way you said it - as if you wanted to tell me but not then. But—"

Nadia looked at Alice as if she was weighing her up. "Nah, Alice. Actually, it weren't so much about what I *was* thinking, as what I *wasn't* thinking."

"*Wasn't* thinking? I don't get it. You said you were happy."

"I was happy. *That's the point,*" Nadia stared across the croquet lawn and batted away a persistent fly. "Look. Listen. Alice, you haven't been up there by the gorge, have you?"

"Can't say I remember ever having been to Bristol," said Alice. "You said it's very high and a long way down but beautiful."

"Exactly. So what do people do in a high up and beautiful place with a sheer cliff edge?" asked Nadia.

"Look, admire the view - a rainbow would be beautiful... maybe wish I had someone to share it with..." Alice looked at her friend, puzzled.

"Nah. Like I said," said Nadia staring straight out in front of her. "You ain't ready."

"How do you know?" responded Alice, a little peeved.

"I'll tell you when, OK?"

Alice said nothing. She looked at her feet.

"I don't mean nothing by it," smiled Nadia, nudging her. "I like you, that's all."

37

Two days later, Bishop Rowena came like a blast of fresh air. Nadia was the first to spot her through the window of the room where they were supposed to be doing their English studies. The bishop strode up to the gates, checked the address and pressed the buzzer.

"Who's that?" wondered Nadia.

Alice leaned over and watched as the gates swung open to admit her. "Dunno."

Bishop Rowena was dressed in a multicoloured sweater and blue jeans. On her feet, she wore a snazzy pair of trainers – or 'sneakers' as she would've called them. Her greying hair, which came to her shoulder blades, was gathered into a simple hairslide.

The woman at the gate was not the person Mrs Brean was warned to expect. Prof W had downloaded a picture of a clergywoman with her hair in a tight bun and wearing a smart dark-coloured trouser suit, high heels, and pink-purple bishop's shirt with clerical collar.

"Hi. Rowena Fontaine," she announced to the quizzical Mrs Brean. "Professor Williams is expecting me... I'm Bishop

Fontaine from America," she added in her New York accent. "I'm supposed to be on holiday and my assistant absolutely forbade me to bring my uniform."

"You'd better come in." Mrs Brean greeted her at the door with a look of barely hidden disdain. In *her* book, bishops were men with educated British accents who were never to be seen without their robes and collars. She was clearly thinking, *Whatever is the world coming to?* "I'll find the professor," she said, curtly.

Rowena's keen ears overheard Mrs Brean saying to her boss in a low voice, "It's her. Looking decidedly scruffy."

Prof W emerged from his study. "Bishop!" he simpered, "Come in. Take a seat. It's very good to see you – and you're on holiday?"

"Thanks. Yeah, I've come to Europe to see family – in France mostly. But I couldn't resist popping in. You see, for me, young people are not just a job."

"Tea? Or coffee perhaps?"

"Oh. Tea. When I'm in London, I want tea. You British know how to make it."

"Mrs Brean, can you get us tea for two? – English Breakfast... unless you would like Darjeeling—"

"Oh, no. The strong sort."

Mrs Brean disappeared to get the tea and as she crossed

the hall she spotted four curious faces on the stairs. "Back to your studies," she ordered. "This is nothing to concern you!"

"Oh yes it is," murmured Hen softly to the others as they regained the landing. "That's Bishop Rowena."

"She doesn't look like a bishop," observed Nadia.

"It doesn't do to typecast. We do too much of that in Britain," pronounced Hen.

Alice smiled. "I thought you were posh, from a traditional school, Hen. I'm still trying to make you out."

"It's all about image. There are lots of people in my school who are not exactly old-type establishment – including staff. We can be quite postmodern; the tea at Wincanton is all fair trade." Nadia had given up trying to follow but Tom was cottoning onto Hen. He kept using big words that made it hard to understand, but he got the drift. He interpreted.

"There are guys at your school who're wiser to the real world than you'd think."

"Exactly," said Hen, glad of someone who understood. "We have an ear for the international scene. That's why my parents chose the school. You can't put all public schools into the same basket."

"Glad to hear it," said Alice. "But, the question now is, will we get to see this cool bishop, or will Prof W keep her to himself?"

"She'll not leave before she sees me," declared Hen confidently. "My parents will want a report - and when she wants to see me, I'll make sure she sees all of us."

In the professor's study, Bishop Rowena was proving she could be as charming as her host. She soon got him talking about his project. Completely unaware that Rowena had a fair knowledge of the issues from her reading and her meeting with Professor Bradford, the director explained that 5D flipping was a real phenomenon caused by a combination of physical brain structure and brain chemistry. He deliberately used technical words like "neuropeptide receptors" and "cytostasis" designed to impress rather than convey knowledge to this long-haired hippy in trainers. No doubt she held some sway in America, where he imagined, wrongfully, that society was less formal; the connection could be useful. As he poured out his apparent enthusiasm to come up with a cure for these sad young people - "perhaps some form of synthesised ribosomal peptide subjected to proteolysis" - it occurred to him that she might even manage to procure him a suitable specimen.

Rowena was egging him on. She wanted to be sure in her own mind that he really was barking up the wrong tree as Professor Bradford claimed.

"Could these... erm, events be down to the, er, 'beyond'; the extra dimensions forcing their way in... from the outside, I mean?" asked Rowena.

"You mean like some supernatural force?" The professor seemed a little wrong-footed. "Some kind of spiritual experience?" he added

"Well, not exactly," explained Rowena. "God lives beyond any physical dimension. Anyone can be Spirit-filled without departing into another dimension. No, I mean, if these other dimensions actually exist, could it be more than brain waves? You make it sound like a mental illness."

"But it *is*, my dear," said Prof W, emphatically. "These young people are ill. You ask them. They are prevented from living normal lives."

"The lives they imagined they would lead?"

The professor lent forward. "Precisely. I have patients here who can no longer do athletics or sit maths examinations, for example. They are disabled. But within a few years, we could have the cure."

"So, how far are you from finding this cure?" asked the bishop. "In their lifetimes?"

Prof W spotted his chance. "Most certainly. This *is* about generations to come, but it is also about my patients now... I am on the point of publishing my paper but there is just one small piece of research I must complete before I do so."

"What is that, professor?"

"I need to do a physical dissection," he said, making sure he used his professional tone. "So far I have not been able to do that where 5D flipping has been confirmed."

"A dissection? An autopsy?"

"Precisely."

"But you said these sufferers are mostly young," protested the bishop. "They don't turn up dead so often, I hope."

"Tragically they may be turning up dead all of the time – more often than is currently believed. But the problem is that their deaths are always ascribed to other factors – mostly accidents. A 5D flip may take these people into danger so they fall or get run over. It is disastrous if they are driving."

"But you can't know which ones are suffering from 5D," stated the bishop.

"Quite. So you see the problem. But as soon as an opportunity arises I can complete my research..." Prof W broke off as Mrs Brean entered with the tea. Bishop Rowena thanked her with a smile that seemed to soften the lady's stern look.

The professor continued, "If you ever come across anything in the States, I can fly out at a moment's notice. In fact, that is the one most important thing you can do to help me... I mean the project."

"Sure," said Rowena. "I can do that. Not that we want anyone to die... Now, thinking of the living, I would love to meet your real live teenagers. The ones that you're studying."

"Of course. I will take you on a tour of the facility here. Then, I hope, you can stay and have lunch with us. At the moment they are engaged in study time – we don't want to see them get behind in their learning," explained the director.

Rowena smiled. "Glad to hear it. Yes, I'd love to see around. And lunch sounds good... but I don't mean to impose upon you."

Prof W replaced his china cup in its saucer. "No problem, bishop. We are pleased to have people take an interest."

Prof W's guard was completely down as they toured the laboratories and Rowena was introduced to the machines that he was so proud of. She witnessed the charts and learned about the weighing-in and routine physical examinations to which the professor's customers were subjected. Bishop Rowena was quite capable of putting herself in the place of the victims – a term she thought appropriate – and imagining their discomfort and loss of dignity, but she didn't show it. The professor was still putting on an act but it was getting thinner as they progressed. He had little idea of the intelligence behind Rowena's casual appearance.

To the young people, however, that same appearance made Rowena seem for real. She spoke gently but formally to them at the lunch table in the professor's presence but then proposed a walk.

"Perhaps you four could show me around the area," she said. "If you're free this afternoon. Introduce me to this part of London."

Prof W was caught totally unaware. It had never occurred to him that this woman would want to take his charges outside of his control. He was lost for exactly what to say and while he was still thinking, mouth half open, Alice spoke.

"Er, we—" She was about to say they didn't know the area either, but Hen guessed what the bishop was about.

"We'd love to!" interjected Hen. "This is a very interesting part of London. We have the Lord's Cricket Ground not too far away... And the leisure centre too."

"Good. That would be fun," responded Rowena. "I have a few things to ask your professor and then we can go if you like. Shall we say, meet in the hall in ten minutes?"

"No problem," said Hen. "Come on guys. Let's get ourselves ready." And he led the others out of the dining room. On the stairs he said, quietly, "I guess Bishop Rowena wants to talk to us somewhere where the doors don't have ears."

Alice was confused. "If she's your dad's friend, Hen, she hasn't said anything. "

"But the prof doesn't know that."

Alice beamed. "She's devious!"

"I would prefer to say she's prudent," laughed Hen.

Tom wondered if that was Christian. "I mean, she is, like, a bishop – even if she doesn't look like one. And she hasn't told the prof the whole truth, has she?"

"Perfectly Christian," reassured Hen. "Jesus told us to be as wise as serpents and innocent as doves. If she told him she knew my dad he would never have let her into his secrets. And he would have been very reluctant to let her talk to us in private."

Alice recognised that she herself had taken to doing exactly the same sort of thing in the clinic. It was like defending your space. Perhaps, if a bishop did it, and if Hen was right and Jesus himself condoned it, it couldn't be so wrong – hardly bad at all.

38

As soon as the four plus the bishop were around the corner, Rowena stopped and smiled. "Hi. What names do you all go by? So far I've only heard your surnames. I'm Rowena."

"Alice." Alice extended a hand.

"Nadia."

"I'm Tom."

"And I'm Christopher," said Hen, crisply.

"Hen," corrected Nadia.

Bishop Rowena began, "Christopher, it's—"

"Hen," interrupted Nadia, again.

Hen nodded ascent, "Bishop, you'd better call me Hen. That's my nickname. Not my choice but there it is."

"Well, if I'm going to call you Hen then I won't take it as disrespectful if you call me Ro."

This was not going to be easy, thought Alice. *I've never called a grown-up by her nickname.* But Ro was treating them as young adults. She wasn't talking down to them. Alice felt ashamed again of the silly childish way she had behaved at the zoo; maybe she had been like that because Old Brean had treated them as children. With Ro it was just the opposite.

"Hen," resumed Ro, "It's your father who is concerned, isn't it?" She used a serious tone that was a million miles away from the sweet notes she employed for the director.

"Yes. My father thought you – or someone in New York could help. Seeing as there is an institute there that is supposed to be like ours."

"There is a facility under the directorship of a Professor Bradford – but it's not at all like yours... Let's find a place to talk. There used to be a Subway on the Finchley Road."

"You said you didn't know this part of London," protested Alice.

"I'm afraid to say I know it quite well. I've been here a lot. I spent some time training over there – Bedford College. It's been a few years, though."

Alice gasped. "You lied!"

"I know. Naughty, aren't I? And I'm afraid I gave completely the wrong impression to your professor about my mission. I'm quite despicable. I'll have to serve a big penance, won't I?" She laughed.

"Wise as a serpent and innocent as a dove," quoted Hen.

"Ah. I see a man who knows his bible. Matthew chapter ten, verse sixteen."

Hen coloured. "No. Not really. I just know that Jesus said

that; I couldn't tell you where it came from."

"I bet you know quite a bit, young man."

"He's clever," explained Nadia, in a matter-of-fact voice.

"I'm impressed with all four of you," complimented the bishop. "Come on, let's see if this Subway is still there."

Ro led them to the Finchley Road past Swiss Cottage and took them into the Subway café.

"Like this stuff?"

Nadia's face lit up. "Yeah. I haven't had this in, like, ages."

"What'll you have? Choose your sub."

"But we've had lunch," protested Alice.

"So you can't eat any more? I don't believe it!"

"I can," declared Nadia.

Soon they were all tucking into subs and Coke.

"I don't mind this stuff," said Hen. "I'm glad it's not cheesy chips. I can't stand cheesy chips."

They all laughed. Hen was one of a rare breed among teenagers. Nadia was enjoying herself so much she thought she was going to flip but she held on. The fear of "losing it" in the fast food joint was enough to stop it.

They began to explain all about the fifth dimension – what happened when they entered a flip, and how it felt. Alice sensed, for the first time in months, that they could speak freely to an adult. What was it about Bishop Rowena that caused them to trust her? If she was a spy for anyone, she was a good one. She was solid and real. She could act a part - she had with the prof - but they were pretty sure she wasn't acting with them. She came over as both genuinely interested and caring. Alice, however, decided on a test question just to make sure.

"Look. You say you're a bishop, right?"

"Yes. I am a bishop," replied Rowena. "Don't I look like one?"

"Well, frankly, no," said Alice. "I've never met a *woman* bishop. How did women get to be bishops? Who was the first one?"

"You're not just asking out of curiosity, right?" Rowena chuckled. She beamed. "You need to know I'm the real McCoy."

"Yeah. We need to know you're genuine. We've never met you before. Answer the question!" Alice spoke rather more sharply than she intended.

Tom apologised. "Alice, that was a bit rude."

"No," said Rowena, "she's right to be careful. You've been lied to too many times. The first female bishop in the Anglican Communion was Barbara Harris. She became a bishop in the diocese of Massachusetts in 1989."

"What's the ninth commandment?" blurted Nadia, not wanting to be left out of the conversation.

Rowena smiled. "You shall not bear false witness against your neighbour."

Nadia looked confused. "My dad says it says, 'Thou shalt not lie'.'"

"That's not a bad way of putting it," agreed Rowena. "It's about making a false statement under oath... er, in a court of law, in the witness box. But there are times when you have to be wise about how much of the truth you share – especially if people are not being straight with you... So let me ask you one, Nadia. What's the fifth commandment?"

Nadia put down her sub and counted on her fingers. "Thou shalt not argue with your parents."

"That'll do. Your dad's got it all worked out, hasn't he? Do you argue with your dad?" asked Rowena, carefully. A large juggernaut roared past the window. It allowed Nadia time to think.

"Not all the time; I only argue when he's drinking too much," she answered, honestly.

"You look after him, don't you?" said Rowena – a look of genuine compassion on her face. Alice thought, *this woman is pretty acquainted with teenagers – she asks the right questions.*

"Yeah, sort of," answered Nadia.

"I think, Nadia, that when you look after your dad, that's when you're *really* obeying the commandment. He should be glad he's got you."

"Yeah. Only, right now, he ain't got nobody, except..." She was going to say, "Except for my phone calls" but stopped herself in time.

"Except?" Rowena felt she needed Nadia to finish her sentence.

"Except he knows I think about him. He knows where I am," Nadia replied truthfully.

"I think he's pretty lucky having you - even if you are in London," assured the bishop.

"Sometimes..." Nadia struggled for the right words, "sometimes I think it's, like, better that I ain't there... I know that sounds stupid."

"No it doesn't," said Rowena. "It means you can tell him you love him without having to make him feel bad about himself when you pick him up off the floor and argue with him for being drunk. He gets all the nice stuff without the guilt."

Nadia was impressed. "You know a lot, don't you? Your dad an alcoholic, too?"

"No. But, sadly, you're not alone in having to cope with a drunken parent," answered Rowena. "And on top of that, Nadia, you have to cope with this 5D thing."

"Yeah. But it's not so bad, really." Nadia, returned to her chicken and bacon ranch melt sub. "It's given me friends; last birthday I got zilch cards, this time I got eight."

"Including one from your dad," put in Alice.

"Yeah," smiled Nadia, oozing sauce from the corners of her mouth. "First time ever."

Rowena changed the mood. "OK. So we need to get this sorted out."

Alice looked at Hen. She thought he should say something here. He'd been quite quiet for a long time but before he could say anything, Nadia swallowed her mouthful, wiped her mouth on the back of her hand and blurted, "The prof's wanting to get his hands on the brain of a flipper to chop it up... But he ain't getting mine!" she added.

"Good," said Ro. "You keep looking after yourself and stay alive, then... Why do you stay? Why don't you all just leave? In fact, you could all get on a train and go home right now. Go home."

They each looked at the others.

"We're researching this," explained Alice. She nudged Hen to say something.

"Erm, yes," said Hen. "Together we can make progress into how to exercise control. Four minds together are better than each of us finding out individually. We are making progress."

Alice became impassioned. "And we need each other because back home no one else knows what it's like... Even my best friend, Becky, hasn't a clue. And Mum and Dad are, frankly, scared... And Tom is worse off than me. And Hen's been chucked out of his school and would have to go and live in the Middle East, and..." she trailed off, feeling a little embarrassed at the strength with which she had spoken.

Hen summed it up. "At this moment we feel safer together. If the prof is after our brains, we just have to look out for each other. He's still got over five months before Padget pulls the plug and if we can keep him sweet, it's much safer for us. Plus, if we weren't together, we'd get nowhere."

"Truth is we aren't sure what would happen to us if we did a bunk," confirmed Tom.

"The prof's scared," explained Hen. "And scared people can be dangerous. So that's why we want allies like you. The best thing we can do is keep him as sweet as possible for as long as possible. November is his deadline."

"We're family, right? We stick together," declared Alice. She raised her right hand in a high five.

Nadia met Alice's hand and then, wham - Nadia was gone. She re-emerged only a second later half under the table, spluttering.

"Sorry," she said, sheepishly. "I panicked."

"Try to keep control next time," said Hen. "You proved you can do it."

"Yeah. Sorry. It caught me by surprise - like, you really mean that, Alice?"

"Yes, Nadia. I do."

"Thanks. That's, like, so cool. Never had a proper family."

Bishop Ro sat motionlessly. This was the first time she had witnessed anyone flipping. "Is this what you guys have to live with all the time? I can see why you want to stay together."

"Yes," nodded Hen, "What we want to do is find a way of controlling it because until we do we can't go anywhere or do anything. People keep sending for ambulances and stuff."

"And that's totally annoying," complained Alice.

"OK, guys. I'm going to do everything I can for you. You're doing well. Keep it up. Hang on in there. We'll try and have this thing sorted well before November. I am going to report this to Professor Bradford. Don't worry, I won't get you into any kind of trouble. Just remember, the world has many good, genuine people who really do care. You will be prayed for every day. I'll put you on the 815 prayer board." The bishop explained about the office in which she worked.

"That sounds cool. New York. I'd love to go there!" Nadia held on, determined not to repeat her flip.

Rowena could see the appeal. "New York's OK. Like every city, there's a lot that's cool and a lot that isn't. When I get back home the young people there will all be envious of me coming all the way to swinging London. But you're right. Having an office so close to institutions like the UN is brilliant. One day, I'll take you there. But, for now, what you have to do is just hang on here. I guess it's boring and not nice most of the time."

"You can say that again," mumbled Alice.

"Be brave," said Rowena. "Remember you have friends out here in the free world... Now, I'm going to give you a way of communicating with me that won't arouse suspicion should your professor monitor your emails."

"He does... All of them, " confirmed Hen.

"I know. Your father has told me, Hen. You and he have devised quite a clever code system. Let me add to it. If you have a real emergency and you need to be got out in a hurry, email me on *rofo@kmail.com*. It's not my usual address – it's a personal private one. Just tell me you're 'dying for cheesy chips'. Use those exact words and I'll know you're in trouble – especially as you hate the things, right?"

"OK. I'm 'dying for cheesy chips'," parroted Hen.

"Yes. Those exact words. If things are OK say: 'The team's scoring well.' And if things are rocky, but you're just about coping say: 'You never know what the weather's going to be like in London.'"

"What if we want some advice – we want to talk to someone?" asked Hen.

The bishop thought. Then said, "How about, 'The lessons are difficult. I need a real teacher'. I might be able to get someone to you – or even come myself, but I can't guarantee that."

Hen wrote it all down on his serviette.

"Don't forget, just tell me your team's doing well every so often," instructed Ro. "If I don't hear from you, I'll come looking for you. No messages and I'll get mobilised. I'll remain in contact with your parents in Abu Dhabi too. The main thing I want you to remember is that you have friends. But just don't let any of this conversation get to your prof. You don't want him to panic. Keep him calm."

Nadia giggled. "Act dumb. Shouldn't be hard. Remember guys, dumb's the word!"

"Exactly," said Ro. "I can see you're actually pretty bright."

"Thanks. You haven't been to my school, Ro. There I'm a natural at being dumb."

"I don't believe that, Nadia. And, anyway, school work isn't everything. The important thing in life is knowing what makes this world really work, and you do."

39

Alice was nominated to be the one to approach Prof W
and ask for another outing. Apparently, she was judged
to be the one with the right kind of guile!

"OK, guys. I'll do it," she agreed, accepting her new-found
talent which she wasn't entirely proud of.

At the first opportunity, Alice asked for a moment with her
professor. She began by saying how important they all felt it
was to stay at the clinic but they were getting bored; teenagers
needed lots of action. She explained that when they were out
with the bishop they had seen a youth club advertised on the
notice board at St Peter's church – the Victorian one with the
solid wooden doors. Could they go along?

Prof W began as if to protest but Alice, expecting this, put
on her most appealing crestfallen look. *If a bishop can use
charm on him, so can I,* she reasoned. He fell for it. Alice
wondered what her parents would think about her learning to
be cunning – perhaps under the circumstances, they would
approve. She hoped so.

The professor said he would look into it.

"It's tomorrow night," said Alice, meekly. "I have the

number to ring right here." She handed him a small piece of paper. She did not move - clearly desiring him to ring the number while she waited. Again, the professor gave in. He didn't want any trouble; he needed to keep them happy.

Someone answered. *Great*, thought Alice. Prof W explained that he had four teenagers at the Winterford who would like to come to the club. He could not guarantee, however, that they wouldn't have a "fit" whilst there. He clearly hoped that they would be turned down.

Alice was about to protest that they did not have "fits". However, the prof's face showed that he wasn't hearing what he wanted. Apparently, the club accepted anyone and everyone. "You have people among your volunteers who can handle fitting? I— You have a doctor. Oh... Yes, I will see they get there. Seven o'clock. Fine... Their names? I will get back to you... within the hour... Goodbye."

"Professor, flipping is not fitting," protested Alice, gently. She had calmed down.

"I know, but how else am I to explain it? But apparently they have a boy who suffers from epilepsy and they weren't put off... You *all* want to go?"

"Yes."

"Tell the others to come and see me - one at a time."

"Fine."

Fifteen minutes later all four were expected at the youth

group the following evening.

☆☆☆

When they got to St Peter's, they were immediately made a lot of fuss of. There were about twenty people all around their age or a bit younger. It was like a blast of fresh air meeting new young people – they hadn't realised just how much they had got used to being isolated. Various young people commented.

"What? You're not allowed phones! No way!"

"Totally out of order."

"How do you live without a phone?"

"What about online games?"

"How do you get to hear any music?"

"No way will you catch *me* in there! It sounds worse than a prison; you can smuggle stuff into a prison."

"Maybe we could smuggle stuff into you..."

"We're not allowed phones," explained Nadia, "but that don't mean I don't have one. I have it to call me dad. No one knows about it. And no one is allowed to call *me*." She didn't want these other kids to feel sorry for her or thinking her a wuss for staying at such a place.

In a moment when the four of them were alone, Alice spoke quietly, "You didn't tell us about a phone, Nadia."

"You didn't ask... Look, it's just for me dad. I have to check on him. I don't want you all using it. That would—"

"Get you caught," finished Hen, in a wise tone. "We'll keep it a secret."

"Thanks. It's not that I don't trust you or anything," she added quickly. "I'm telling these guys because I don't want them to feel sorry for me."

The group was fun. They were in the middle of a noisy floor hockey match when the leader called over to Nadia.

"Nadia, someone's come for you."

40

Earlier that evening, Prof W had hardly got back from taking his charges to the youth group when a plain white van pulled up to the gates of the Winterford clinic. A burly man got out and entered the code on the keypad. The gates swung open and the van drove up to the house. Donald Padget was out of the passenger seat before the driver – a stark contrast to the way he had arrived the previous time. Padget strode up to the main entrance of the clinic, his face set with a no-nonsense expression. He pulled the handle that clanged his presence.

Prof W went to open the door. He had seen the van but he had no idea that the person tugging the bell pull was the last person he wanted to see; he was still basking in the comfort of the young people's being nice to him and showing their appreciation for being allowed out. He opened the door and his jaw almost fell on his boots; he was both shocked and scared.

"Time's up," announced Padget. He pushed the door wide.

"But... but you said November!"

"Changed my mind. Have you got a brain yet?"

"N...no. I was hoping... but... no. Not yet. But I hope to

have soon – I have established new contacts... international ones. The net is spread widely. You can–"

"No more dilly-dallying, Williams. If you had a brain tomorrow, how long would it take you to make your breakthrough?"

"Well, it would depend on the brain... If I find what I'm looking for... What I expect to find."

"And if you do?"

"L...less than a month. I have the paper almost completed. All I need is the physical proof... Then, it will take up to three months for the publication in the *Lancet* or the *British Medical Journal*. It will have to be peer reviewed before it is published, and–"

"I don't care about your paper, professor. When will you know the answer? When will *you* know how this fifth dimension thing works?"

"In the autopsy itself, of course, but the recording process takes–"

"What do you need to perform an autopsy?"

"The usual things. The dissecting instruments, the machine I use for preparing slides... and the microscope is vital."

"Where are they?"

The professor was now getting properly frightened. Donald Padget looked ready to do anything if he did not comply.

"I... In the lab," he stammered. "But, as I said, I don't have a specimen, yet."

Padget helped himself to the whiskey in the bottom drawer.

"I'll say this for you, Williams, you have a good taste in whiskey... A specimen? For an intelligent man, Williams, you are singularly short of imagination."

"What? ..." blustered the professor. His mouth hung open.

"Come now. Time to collect our brain," said the entrepreneur, with false amusement.

"What? Where?" The professor was now terrified.

"Which one do you reckon would make the best subject, Williams?"

"What? What are you—"

"Of your four teenagers, professor," said Padget, with an exasperated sigh, "which one?"

Professor Williams made a desperate last attempt at trying to deny the implications of what the financier was saying. "They are all in excellent health, I assure you," he blustered.

"Good. So no complications then. Fresh and clean."

There was now no avoiding the man's intentions. "You don't mean?—" began the professor.

Padget smirked. "Oh, yes I do, professor. Don't tell me you haven't longed for one of them to have an accident! I'm just offering you the opportunity."

"But that's m—"

"That's life or death professor. Which one?"

"I couldn't possibly—"

"Which one professor?" demanded Padget impatiently with force. "How far are you willing to go to secure your clinic – I own it in all but name? What about the Nobel prize professor? How far are you willing to go?"

"Murder is illegal. An accident is one thing, but murder! What if the police... impossible to cover up," attempted the professor. "No. Not possible."

"So," Padget stared him in the eye and kept walking forward as the director stepped backwards against his bookshelves. "I'm sorry to have to put it this way, Williams." He lowered his voice, his face just inches from the professor's. "You would be a great loss to the scientific establishment, but..." He backed off, leaving Prof W flattened against his books.

Padget helped himself to another shot of whiskey. Gesturing with his glass, he said calmly, "I mean what I say; it's life or death – for *you*. I'm afraid it's *you* or *them*...

Padget indicated his chauffeur. "Mr Wood, here," he said, "is quite capable of seeing that you have a 'terminal event' in that canal down the road. Of course, we'll make it look like a suicide. Did you know I have a boat in Little Venice? Nice spot. Which one, Williams? Decide now. My men are ready for you—"

"OK. OK," panicked the professor. He did not doubt that Padget and his heavy were capable of murder. "They're all at the youth club up the road."

"I know that, Williams, we watched you take them... Last time, professor. Which one?"

"N... Nadia Simpson. She has the most pronounced episodes," gasped Prof W.

Donald Padget poured a glass of whiskey and held it out for the professor. "One for the road, Williams? You take it straight?" he drawled. Prof W took the glass and gulped down the contents.

"Oh come on, professor. Drinking it like that is quite a waste," mocked Padget. "Wood will follow you as you drive your car to the church hall. You will call for Nadia Simpson and tell her her mother – she has a mother I assume – is in trouble... oh, professor," simpered Padget as he saw the alarm on Williams' face, "it's just a story. Nothing has happened to the mother, but the girl will follow you. Kids seem to have some kind of attachment to their mothers. She has got a mother, I take it?"

"No. A father – about her only relative," stammered the professor.

"Perfect," smiled Padget. "Her father, then. So she'll come quickly and quietly and won't muck about attracting too much attention. When you have brought her here we'll all go for a long drive in the van ... oh, professor, you didn't believe me when I said I had a boat in Little Venice, did you? Do you really think you would catch me on a houseboat? Just a joke, professor." Wood laughed and Padget smiled, broadly. Then his face changed. "Time to go," he said, sharply. "And no funny business! Wood will follow you in the van."

41

In the youth club, Nadia came up to Alice, Tom and Hen to say that the prof had come for her. Her dad had had an accident - she had to go. She told the youth leader that the club was cool and she wanted to come again when she got back.

"I ain't going to hang around unless he's real bad," she assured her friends. "But he needs to know that I know and that I care. See ya." The young people each gave her a hug and then she was gone.

"OK. So what's happened to me dad?" demanded Nadia, as she got into the prof's car.

"An accident," replied the professor. He was sweating. *He must have been running*, thought Nadia. He caught his breath. "I... I don't know the details," he stammered. "I'll take you back to the clinic and you can collect a few things and we'll take you straight to Bristol."

As the gates to the clinic opened to admit them, Nadia saw a white van draw up behind them but didn't give it much thought. Prof W parked his car and Nadia got out and waited for him to unlock the front door. Inside the hallway, they were greeted by Padget. Nadia was instantly aware that something was wrong – Prof W had been edgy and nervous ever since he had picked her up and now she was positively alarmed.

"What's up?!" she demanded.

"All right, g... gentleman," spluttered Prof W trying to keep calm but failing. "If you would like to wait in my o... office."

"No time for the niceties," growled Padget and grabbed Nadia's upper arm violently. "Get it done!"

Nadia pulled away from him. "What the bleedin' 'ell's goin' on?!" she yelled, instinctively pulling her arm free and backing away out of the front door. Wood sneered and made a lunge for her. Burning with anger, Nadia sidestepped him. "You b–" she began but then her world turned upside down and she was flipping – more violently than she could ever remember doing before.

Inside the fifth, Nadia instinctively began overtaking the ellipses and running up the slope – anything to delay her entry and maybe re-enter the 4D world somewhere else. Adrenaline surged through her. Whatever was going on was wrong. Padget was evil and she realised that the prof was scared – terrified. She guessed – she hoped – the stuff about her dad and an accident was all a rouse to get her away from the others.

Nadia's concentration was intense and she found herself higher up the slope beyond the balls than she had ever been.

The top of the slope seemed almost in reach. Beyond it, the grey gave way to the palest of blues – like the early morning of a clear blue sky before the sun has actually topped the horizon. Nadia clawed her way to the ridge that marked the top of the slope and then, at last, she made it. It was narrow – very narrow – because beyond it was a second slope that descended the other side. It was also forty-five degrees from the vertical. She passed her leg over the right angle that formed the apex and breathed. This was new – all new. She saw the vortex on her side way down at the bottom of the incline and now she could see a second at the base of this new slope. *Where*, she thought, *would I come out if I went through that right-hand whirlpool?*

Nadia thought of her friends; she hated the idea of leaving them. As soon as she was out of the fifth, she would head back to the youth club and they could all do a bunk to safety somewhere. She felt a blast of pride now she could report to Hen that she had scaled the slope and found the top – even if it wasn't that brilliant beyond it. It was just the same – grey and empty.

☆☆☆

Oblivious to all that was happening to Nadia, Alice, Hen and Tom stayed at the youth club for the remainder of the evening.

The leader reported to everyone that Nadia had had to go because she had had some bad news about her father, but that she said that she wanted to come again when she got back to London. They said prayers together and included one for Nadia's dad.

At nine o'clock it was time to go. It was Mrs Brean who collected them. She explained that Prof W had phoned her and asked her to pick them up. "He has been exceptionally kind and has taken Nadia to Bristol to see her father," she told them. "Your professor is such a kind and generous man. He did not need to drive all that way, himself. You have a very gracious man in the professor," she said, proudly. And then added, "He spoils you far too much."

42

Nadia sat astride the apex of the fifth-dimensional world and relaxed. She took stock of her situation. At least she was safe here from Padget and his heavy. *I must remember this*, she thought. *Hen will want to know every detail.* Hen was right, there were at least another three dimensions of space inside the so-called fifth – she had discovered a second slope at right angles to the first.

Then she asked herself what Hen would do next if he were there. The question now was whether it would be better to drop onto this new side or descend the slope on her original side and leave through the usual vortex. The thought of Padget and Wood waiting for her made up her mind for her. She did not know what they intended but whatever it was, it was not going to be nice.

Nadia brought her left leg over the top and allowed herself to slide down the alternative incline a little. Soon she was halfway down the slope and realised she would not have the energy to get back up; she was committed. But she didn't want to change her mind. She made a controlled approach to the alternative whirlpool on her right and allowed herself to pass gently through it.

Checking her surroundings, Nadia realised she was across the road from the clinic. To her relief, the white van was not there; she must have managed a time shift as well as a spatial one. Good. She needed to find her friends. They would still be in the youth club - Hen had said you could travel forward no more than half an hour.

Nadia picked her way back through the streets until she found the main road and the church. But when she got there the place looked different. Instead of the notice announcing it to be St Peter's church hall, there was a big board painted black with the words: "Hitler Youth" and a red square enclosing a white circle with a blue swastika in its centre! Nadia thought this bizarre; some pretty gifted graffiti artist was going just too far. Banksy, the noted secret graffiti artist from Bristol, she thought, would never approve.

Some young people passed her but the group seemed to have already dispersed and there was no sign of her three friends. Nadia felt a tinge of panic. She was alone in a strange London street in the late evening with nowhere to go - there was no way she could go back to the clinic. *What the hell am I going to do?* she wondered, feeling suddenly cold. At the clinic, she had been angry, then scared and then relieved when she had got outside and away from that awful man. Now she felt scared again. She had no idea what to do next.

Nadia Simpson, get a grip, she told herself. Then she thought of the Subway place. If they had got out early, her friends might have headed there; it might be open late. She headed up the Finchley Road in the direction she knew it must be.

But everything was different. She couldn't find the café. *Perhaps it's closed,* she told herself. And she looked again at the places in darkness but there was no Subway; in fact, it didn't look like the same street at all. Was she lost? Panicking now, she went back down to the church. No, she was definitely in the right place. Then she noticed that the traffic was subtly different, too, and the few people who bustled along sometimes stared at her. A few women dressed in long skirts hurried passed; they avoided her as if she had some kind of plague. Was it what she was wearing? Nadia had never felt she stood out - she hardly ever wore anything but her jeans and trainers and some kind of top. The way these people were looking at her now was something she had not really encountered before.

Then she realised that it wasn't just her clothes - she was the only black person around. All of the other people she passed were white. That, too, was weird; at least two-thirds of the youth group were non-white. She knew that London was no different from Bristol in that respect - they were both multicultural cities. But these people were checking her out as if she had dropped from outer space. *So what now?* she asked herself. *Hide... and think. I'll flip and come out somewhere else. Better luck, like, next time, girl.* She ducked down an alley and set about trying to bring it on. But the kind of scared she was feeling was the kind that prevented her from flipping. The fear she had felt in front of Padget was thickly coated in hot anger and with more than a tinge of panic. This was different; it was a paralysing fear. She could not summon any of the energy she required.

Then, all of a sudden, out of a doorway, a slight figure appeared. It grabbed hold of Nadia's arm and tugged her further down the alley.

The shock momentarily prevented her from reacting but she was on the point of releasing a torrent of unsavoury language when she recognised the figure – Roxanne!

The story continues in books two and three of the
Flip Trilogy:

1. *Flip! On the Edge*
2. *Beyond the Horizon*
3. *The Daisychain.*

If you have enjoyed this book, please recommend it
to your friends
and rate it on Goodreads:
https://www.goodreads.com

and on Amazon:
https://www.amazon.co.uk/s?k=trevor+stubbs

If you can write a short review, too,
that would be brilliant.

Trevor Stubbs
www.trevorstubbs.co.uk

FROM THE AUTHOR

Between 2008 and 2011, I spent more than two years working in Bishop Gwynne College in Juba in what is now South Sudan.

Next door to the college is a facility for girl street children – Confident Children out of Conflict*. The project grew from small beginnings when groups of girls living rough in the market attached themselves to a few caring people.

Children on the streets – especially girls – are very vulnerable, particularly in the hours of darkness. Although the temperature at night in Juba is relatively benign, virtually nothing else is.

The CCC compound has room for fifty girls but it is well over-subscribed. The aim is to see that the children receive trauma-care, security and the love they so desperately need, as well as proper food, clothing, medical care and school fees.

CCC relies entirely on charitable giving with grants from UNICEF and other trusts and gifts from individuals.

I give all profits from the sale of my books to CCC and I am delighted to report that these, plus other donations that I have received over the years, have resulted in my being able to send them a few thousands of British pounds.

My hope is that with the publication of this Flip trilogy, I will have even more to contribute.

Thank you for your contribution through the purchase of this book.

Trevor Stubbs. July 2019

*www.confidentchildren.org

The White Gates Adventures

by Trevor Stubbs

The Kicking Tree
Ultimate Justice
Winds and Wonders
The Spark

Meet Jack Smith (18) from Planet Earth - angry and drifting -
and Jalli Rarga (17) from Planet Raika in the Andromeda
Galaxy, struggling to be different from other girls.

**Step with them through strange white gates
into wonderful new worlds.**

Adventure - Sci-Fi - Fear - Fun - Humour - Love
**Explore outwards to the vast universe and
inwards into the human heart where everyone matters.**

REVIEWS FOR THE KICKING TREE

"I think this book is amazing. I like the fact that almost nothing bad happens, but that you still want to read more. It is hard to put away and there is not a sentence in the book that is boring."

Ebba (Goodreads)

"This book is one of the most special books I've ever read. In a good way. It's a love story. But it's not really a love story - it's about two people falling love. It's an SF book. But it's not really an SF book: there is some time (perhaps wormhole?) travelling going on and there are spaceships. It's also a fantasy story. But it's not really a fantasy story..."

Lynn (Goodreads)

"Wonderful story. It's a great adventure that made me cry. I love the two main characters who meet across the universe..."

Miss S (Amazon)

"... a perfect book for the adult-literacy teacher trying to encourage teens to read, with it's strong narrative structure, simple vocabulary and positive, active role models. There are all too few authors who write well for this market, and Stubbs is one of them."

Church Times

"Trevor Stubbs has an interesting philosophy of life: 'I hate injustice and oppression, especially against the weak and the vulnerable and want to speak out.' Trevor uses his undoubted skills as a master storyteller and a magical weaver of tales to bring about such justice."

That's Book and Entertainment